Life Ghost On

THE GHOST DETECTIVE MYSTERIES - BOOK 9

JANE HINCHEY

BP · BAYWOLF PRESS · BAYWOLF PRESS

To Kade, whose life was a tale cut short but whose spirit continues to touch hearts. This story is a tribute to your name and the light you brought into the world.

When 'I Do' Turns Into 'Whodunnit?'

Wedding planning is tough, but it's even harder when you're a PI investigating a high-stakes murder. The moment a model turns up dead at the bridal expo, my to-do list gets a lot more complicated.

As if finding a new venue weren't urgent enough —thanks to a fire that turned our dream location into a smoky ruin—I've also got some rather insistent ghosts clamoring for resolution.

Now, here I am, piecing together betrayals, secrets, and a list of suspects as varied as my wedding playlist, and time is running out.

With matrimony and mystery both on the line, the stakes couldn't be higher. In this deadly game of vows and villains, will I make it to "I do," or will 'til death do us part' become all too literal?

Dive into a world where wedding veils and police tape go hand-in-hand. Will you RSVP to this unmissable mystery?

CHAPTER ONE

Two words strike fear into my very soul. *Bridal Expo*. Don't get me wrong, I'm not against them per se, but when I'm the bride-to-be, and my entire family wants to be involved? Yeah, that's a hard no thank-you-very-much.

Seb, my charming, unbelievably good-looking neighbor, hammered the nail into that particular coffin, and I'd crumbled, caved, and given in with undoubtedly lousy grace. He is, after all, my wedding planner, and while I get the final say on everything, Seb overruled me on this one.

"Oh, come on," Seb nudged me with his elbow. "Cheer up; it won't be that bad."

"I just don't see the point," I pouted. "My

wedding is in two days, Seb. *Two days!* What could I possibly need from this expo? I have my dress, I have a venue, I have flowers, a photographer and a cake. So *why* are we here?" My voice sounded like a whiny three-year-old, and I didn't care.

"We're here because you promised me an expo, and since we missed the one in the city because I caught Covid, this is the next best thing!" Seb flashed his pearly whites and danced ahead, waving his arm toward the huge banner stretched across the front of Firefly Bay's town hall announcing the expo.

"Have expo will travel," Laura grinned, taking his place by my side and looping her arm through mine, urging me forward.

"It will be lovely," Mom agreed, coming up on my other side. "I'm looking forward to the fashion parade and seeing all the dresses."

"But I already have my dress," I wailed.

"It doesn't hurt to look," Mom hushed me, while Amanda, trailing behind us, added, "No one is saying you have to change your dress, Audrey. Mind you, you might want to take it easy on the snacks."

My head swiveled around so fast I gave myself whiplash. "What does that mean? Are you saying I'm fat?"

She didn't deny it. Instead, she looked me up and

down thoroughly before shrugging and saying, "I'm saying I'd skip the free treats today if I were you."

"Seriously, Amanda, shut up, you're not helping," Laura snapped, patting my arm soothingly.

"Girls, girls," Seb snapped his fingers, drawing our attention, "Today is about fun. It's not about pressure. Audrey, you gorgeous thing, you don't need to make any decisions today—see? Consider it my gift to you. Just look at all the pretty things, and if you see a tiara you like? Let me know." He winked, a huge, exaggerated wink, and I couldn't help but laugh. Seb had been trying to convince me I needed a tiara, and I steadfastly disagreed.

"Right? Right! Let's go!"

We followed Seb through the doors and found ourselves instantly transported to another world. It was rather magical once you overcame the sheer amount of noise assaulting your ears. The town hall was decked out like a wedding venue, with vast swathes of fabric draped across the ceiling, fairy lights, and flowers everywhere. Vendors had tables sprucing their wares, from makeup stations to stationery, florists, and jewelers. If it were even remotely connected to the wedding industry, it was here.

The tables were arranged in a grid pattern with a

signpost at each row with cute names like 'Honeymoon Lane' and 'First Kiss Boulevard.' They had erected a catwalk at the far end of the hall, extending off the stage. And just like that, my irritation slipped away to be replaced with something suspiciously like excitement.

"See?" Seb slung an arm around my shoulders and squeezed. "It's not so bad. We all like pretty things. Am I right, or am I right? Now, where are all those hunky groom models hiding out?"

"Wait!" I grabbed his arm to stop him from moving away. "Where are you going?"

"Girl, divide and conquer!" He smiled, almost blinding me with his white teeth, but then he must've glimpsed the panic that flashed across my face, for he sobered. "Gather around, ladies," he demanded, maneuvering us into a circle. "Here's the plan. Laura, we need more ribbon, anything in the soft green range."

"Got it," Laura saluted him, and I eyed her suspiciously. Did they all have assignments? Had they been plotting behind my back?

"Amanda, earrings. Something with a sparkle but not too long or flashy. She'll only end up ripping her earlobe off with them. But not too dainty, either."

"Understood." Amanda nodded.

They *had* been plotting behind my back, the sneaky, conniving devils. There was no stopping the smile that curled my lips. It takes brass balls and a poker face to deceive me, and I can't decide whether I want to throttle them or buy them a drink.

"And of course, Mom, we know you're here for the fashion, so we'll all meet at the catwalk at two. Synchronize watches."

"Wait, what are you looking for?" I asked before he could leave.

"Why an eligible bachelor, of course," Seb winked and, with a wave, was immediately swallowed by a sea of white—lace, silk, tulle, off in search of a husband for himself. Or a tiara. Possibly both. I suspected that by the end of the day, I'd be wearing a crown, and the truth was, I'd go along with it because he was Seb, and despite only being my neighbor for a short time, he was fast becoming a solid friend. That and he was the only one, aside from my fiancé, Kade Galloway, who knew that I could see and speak to ghosts. And my cat, Thor. And raccoon, Bandit. It wasn't much, right? Talking to ghosts and animals?

"The look on your face says it all, Fitz." Ben suddenly appeared beside me, accompanied by his usual spectral chill. "Never thought I'd see the day you'd be at a wedding expo." His eyes caught the banners overhead that read "Say 'I do' to your dream wedding" and "The Best Day of Your Life."

"Why am I not surprised to see you here?" I muttered out of the corner of my mouth. Ben was an unashamed, avid fan of the shopping channel and would travel around the neighborhood at all hours of the day—or night—to visit with whoever had his favorite channel playing.

"What's that, love?" Mom turned to me, having caught my mumbling. Ben grinned, then disappeared into the crowd, leaving me to explain why I was talking to myself. Again.

Thinking on my feet, I blurted, "This is overwhelming."

She patted my arm reassuringly. "Oh, darling, it's all part of the fun. You only get married once, you know."

"Statistically speaking, that's not accurate," Amanda chimed in.

Laura shot her a look. "Let's just enjoy the expo, stats aside."

As we weaved through vendors offering everything from cake tastings to honeymoon getaways, I felt a familiar chill that had nothing to do with wedding jitters. Thinking Ben had returned from his sojourn around the venue, I turned to him, mouth open, to ask if he'd seen anything he liked, only to snap it shut just as fast. It wasn't Ben. It was Emily Carson.

"Last minute wedding prep?" she asked, her ethereal form shimmering amid the chaos.

Letting the others surge ahead, I deliberately slowed my pace to talk to Emily. Oddly, she kinda fit in at the expo in her pristine white bridal gown, her auburn hair swept up in an elegant up-style, a silver locket around her neck. I ignored the red stain on the front of her dress, the gaping hole in her abdomen, and that she was incorporeal.

Pulling out my phone, I pretended to take a call.

"Emily, what are you doing here?" I asked, still baffled by the randomness of her visits. "I mean, I haven't seen you in ages." Emily had first appeared when Kade and I had returned from Chicago after visiting his parents. That had been weeks ago. She'd been coming and going ever since.

Emily smirked, her ethereal form shimmering a little. "I'm not tied to Firefly Bay. I go where the wind —or whatever it is that moves us ghosts—takes me."

"And you chose today of all days. While I'm at a bridal expo?" It couldn't be a coincidence, not when she died modeling a bridal gown. What I'd learned about Emily Carson was very little. She was a slender woman with a willowy frame that made her perfect model material. Almond-shaped hazel eyes with a porcelain complexion and a smattering of freckles across her nose and cheeks. She was, in a word, stunning, so it was no surprise she'd turned to modeling.

"Even spirits get curious," she said, glancing at a mannequin dressed in a wedding gown. "So, how's my murder investigation coming along?"

The question wasn't unexpected. "You have no idea how tangled this thing is, Emily. I've pored over public records, stalked social media accounts, and even had run-ins with some less-than-helpful police about your case. And you know what I've got? Zilch. It's like your killer vanished into thin air even before you actually vanished into thin air."

Emily nodded, her eyes softening. But even spectral expressions are telling, and I couldn't miss the glimmer of disappointment in her gaze. "I understand. Life's obstacles aren't just for the living, apparently," she said. Her hand fluttered over her abdomen, where her untimely demise was painfully visible. "Just remember, I can't cross over until this is sorted."

I felt a pang of guilt, like a splinter I couldn't quite dig out. "I'm well aware, and it eats at me, Emily. When the wedding whirlwind dies down, I'll revamp my efforts. Willow Creek won't know what hit it," I promised, pondering if a honeymoon could double as an investigative road trip. Kade might just go for it.

She looked at me, stunningly beautiful. "I'm counting on you, Audrey." Then, just like that, she was gone.

Her absence magnified my guilt. There were scant details to work on—her lifeless body was discovered in a mansion in Willow Creek, wearing the same wedding dress from her last photoshoot. The mansion's owner, a wealthy philanthropist named George Dawson, disappeared a week after Emily's body was found. Suspected but never proven guilty. Another dead-end in a case full of them.

A hand wrapped around my wrist and jerked me forward, pulling me from my thoughts. "Come on, Audrey, let's stick together," Laura said. "Can't have you sneaking out on us."

The hours passed surprisingly quickly, and before I knew it, we were on our way to the catwalk,

Mom practically buzzing with excitement. They'd already had several sessions featuring bridesmaid and flower girl outfits, but two o'clock was the grand finale, the wedding gowns.

Laura carried a tote bag stuffed with ribbons and tulle of varying shades of green and pink, Amanda had snagged the perfect earrings, and I'd sampled almost every cake that was on offer—so much so that my stomach hurt—and I'd locked eyes with Amanda over every mouthful. To give her credit, she didn't say a word, although her lips had thinned into a straight line, a sure sign of her disapproval.

I'd only knocked over one candle, thankfully not alight, which was a definite win because I'm the clumsiest person I know. We'd stopped by a table with an elaborate display of tiaras and veils and had discussed my decision to veto a veil—too risky. I'd either step on it, shut it in a door, or some other situation was bound to crop up where I'd end up ripping it off my head. Plus, a veil was a step too far in the direction of formal, which was not what I wanted.

Kade and I wanted our wedding to be fun, not formal. Yes, I'd be in a magnificent white dress—A *Lise Magnier* A-line gown featuring sparkling, beaded floral lace over a plunging v-shaped neckline and a hidden thigh-high slit under a layer of shimmering tulle. The moment the saleswoman had slipped it over my head, I'd been mesmerized. I'd said yes to the dress.

Kade would be in tan chinos with a matching waistcoat and a white button-down with the sleeves rolled up. Our reception was in a barn, and while our cake was three tiers, it was decorated with a cute country vibe with green vines, pastel roses, and wildflowers, and the bottom tier had a cute wooden fence. Everything was rustic, country, low-key, and one hundred percent us.

"Come, come," Seb hurried up, ushering us towards seats in the front row. "I reserved these for us."

Mom almost flattened me in her stampede to get the best seat. She needn't have worried. All the seats had the best view.

"How did you manage this?" I asked, waiting for Amanda and Laura to proceed me before taking my seat.

"Oh, I know a guy who owed me a favor." Seb winked, and my mind boggled with possibilities. By day, Seb was a schoolteacher. By night? Well, besides being a marriage celebrant—mostly for same-sex couples—he also made an amazing wedding planner. A role I'd gladly handed over to him when he'd offered.

"Shush," he grabbed my hand. "It's starting."

Models began floating down the runway in dreamy gowns that probably cost more than my car. Each dress seemed more intricate than the last— swaths of lace, dramatic veils, delicate beadwork, and flowing trains.

"That one's gorgeous," Laura pointed out, her eyes locked on a mermaid-style gown that seemed painted on the model.

"Yeah, but not practical. Poor girl can hardly walk," Amanda weighed in.

I was about to agree when another dress caught my eye. It was a classic A-line with lace sleeves, similar to the one I'd picked. "What about that one?"

Mum nodded, clearly pleased. "That's more like it." She leaned over and whispered, "It even has the perfect inner lining for the hidden pocket tradition."

I chuckled. "You're still on about that, huh?"

Her smile was warm, almost wistful. "You'll see. With that little token tucked away on your wedding day, you'll feel the generations of love and good luck we've sewn into our family's fabric. Literally."

We sat in the front row, enthralled, as tall, willowy models glided along the catwalk, modeling the wedding dresses. They were unique and beautiful, and I'd been quietly worried I'd have buyer's remorse over my dress, but hallelujah, I didn't see a dress I liked more. I'd even relaxed back into my seat, legs outstretched and crossed at the ankles, enjoying the show when Seb grabbed my arm, making me jump.

"This is the grand finale," he whispered. "Behind that curtain is a B.I.G. huge wedding cake, and on top of it is model extraordinaire Rayna Mills in a gold gown."

"How do you know all of this?"

"It's my mission to know. Plus, I hung out at the back; it took me all of ten minutes to pick up the goss."

"And the goss is?"

"Gossip, darl," He shot back without looking at me.

I snorted. "I know what goss means. But what did you find out? What is the gossip?"

"Oh, the usual, Rayna has top billing, but another model, Nicole, is ... let's just say a tad annoyed she didn't get the top job, so the atmosphere in the dressing room is a smidge on the frosty side."

Mum leaned in, her voice tinged with

excitement. "That dress is supposed to be the highlight of the show, you know. They say the designer is here. What's her name, Marigold something?"

"Marianne Thompson," Seb replied, not taking his eyes from the stage. He was practically on the edge of his seat in anticipation. "She started her boutique five years ago and has been moderately successful—her bridal designs have been featured in a few local magazines."

"You know her?" I asked.

"Not personally, but I'm angling for an introduction after the big reveal." Before he could continue, the lights dimmed, and a hush fell over the crowd, replaced by the rich crescendo of orchestral music. A single spotlight focused on the curtain.

The MC's voice filled the room. "Ladies and gentlemen, prepare yourselves for the pièce de résistance!"

With that, confetti cannons boomed, showering us all in a glittery haze. Amidst the explosion of sound and color, I thought I heard something else— a sharp, discordant noise that felt out of place, and I half wondered if someone had dropped something backstage, but in the chaos of the moment, I dismissed it.

The curtain lifted slowly, revealing the gargantuan wedding cake. But it wasn't the cake that caught everyone's attention. It was Rayna Mills, the model who was supposed to embody the epitome of bridal splendor in her gold wedding dress. She was there, lying motionless atop the cake, her dazzling gown marred by a dark, spreading stain.

Gasps echoed through the room, replacing the music that had so joyously filled the air moments before. Time seemed to freeze as everyone processed the horrifying spectacle before us.

The screaming was not unexpected. Not by Rayna. She remained motionless atop the cake. No, the screaming came from models standing in the wings who rushed onto the stage, all looking up at Rayna in horror. Standing sentinel at the base of the cake, the groomsmen looked confused, then they, too, looked up at Rayna and started yelling for a medic.

"What's happened?" Laura asked. "Has she fainted? I wouldn't be surprised, squeezing in and out of those big heavy gowns."

Then Rayna moved. Grabbing handfuls of the shimmering gold fabric, she hiked it up and stood, awkwardly making her way off the cake when no one helped her.

"You guys! You're ruining EVERYTHING!" she screamed, stomping a foot. "Why are you doing this to me?" Only, of course, no one heard her, no one except me, because Rayna Mills was dead and I was seeing her ghost.

CHAPTER TWO

The room erupted into chaos, and Seb ushered us from our seats. The commotion grew louder, with people shrieking and rushing towards the exits. Mom grabbed my arm, her eyes wide with shock. "Audrey, we need to get out of here." She dragged me halfway across the floor before I dug my heels in, forcing her to stop.

"I know, Mom, but I left my purse at our seats. My phone, my keys, everything's in there," I lied, my eyes flitting back to Rayna's furious ghost, visible only to me, having a meltdown near her lifeless body. I couldn't ignore her. "I have to go get it. You go ahead, I'll catch up."

"Are you sure it's safe?" Laura looked alarmed, her eyes scanning the panicking crowd.

"I'll be quick," I promised, hating the lie but knowing I couldn't leave. Not yet. I looked at Rayna's pacing figure and thought about the ramifications of ignoring her. If I didn't help her, she'd probably manifest in my living room, prancing around like it was her personal runway. I sighed; my impending nuptials were stressful enough without throwing a spectral bridal diva into the mix.

And then, as if summoned by the thought of bridal chaos, Emily Carson shimmered into existence beside me. Emily gave me an empathetic look as if to say, "You too, huh?"

I groaned internally. With Emily's sporadic visits, Rayna's newfound non-living status, and Ben's sarcastic but comforting presence, my house had the potential to turn into America's Next Top Ghost Model. The last thing I needed was for my home to become a spectral stage for deceased brides battling for the limelight.

"Look, ladies," I could imagine Ben quipping, "Audrey's the only bride we have room for here. You both look fabulous, really, but one's romantic, two's a haunting, and three's a crowd."

Deciding that a ghostly Bridezilla standoff was a subplot my life definitely didn't need right now, I made up my mind. Investigating Rayna's murder became a non-negotiable—for her, Emily, and my teetering sanity. Pushing aside the adrenaline surge, the almost intoxicating thrill of hunting a killer, I refocused. *This is for Rayna*, became my convenient little lie.

Seeing my determined expression, Laura finally nodded. "All right, but hurry."

They reluctantly made their way to the exit, blending into the crowd of people. As soon as they were out of sight, I took a deep breath and maneuvered through the disarray, heading toward the stage. My focus wasn't on a misplaced purse but a restless spirit who didn't even realize she was a spirit yet.

I made my way up the stairs at the side of the stage and slipped behind the heavy curtain, everyone too busy to notice me, paying me no heed. Rayna looked surprised to see me, unaware of her lifeless body only feet away atop that grand cake.

Pulling out my phone, I held it to my ear and pretended to be on a call as I approached her. "You need to follow me," I said. "I can't talk here."

Rayna stopped her stomping, and our eyes met. "Are you talking to me?"

"Yes."

"Why are they all ignoring me?" She wailed,

waving her arm to indicate her fellow models who were distracted with ... well, Rayna's lifeless body. A body Rayna's spirit had failed to notice.

"It's a bit loud where I am," I said into the phone. "I'm going to find somewhere a little quieter, where I can hear you better." I headed further backstage, away from the ruckus.

Rayna's ghost followed, her rant continuing. "I can't believe they ruined my moment! It was supposed to be perfect!"

I kept my face neutral as I navigated the labyrinth backstage, doing my best to ignore Rayna's rant about her sabotaged big moment. If she thought this was bad, wait until she realized she was dead!

"Oh, look at that!" Rayna exclaimed, pointing at a mirror that caught her ghostly reflection. "My makeup's a train wreck! This is a disaster."

"Rayna," I hissed, trying to keep my voice down, "You're dead. There's a bit more to worry about here." I grimaced at my lack of tact; so much for easing her into the whole being-dead thing.

She stopped and turned to me, her face a mask of disbelief. "Dead? Don't be absurd. I was just on stage, and everything was going perfectly until..."

She trailed off, her hand moving to her chest, where a dark, ghostly hole became more apparent.

"Oh," she said, her voice small. "Oh, I see."

As realization settled in, the petulant brat vanished, replaced by a frightened young woman who had just come to terms with her murder.

"What do we do now?" Rayna asked, her voice quivering.

I looked at her, knowing I was probably stretching myself too thin by getting involved with her death so close to my wedding, but unable to help myself. "We find out who did this to you."

"Is this because of the note?" she sniffed.

"Note? What note?"

"I found a note this morning. I thought it was from one of the others, pulling some prank."

"Show me."

Rayna brushed past me, leaving a ghostly chill in her wake. I followed her to the dressing room and opened the door. The room was eerily empty, clothes flung about, the scene unnervingly chaotic.

"Is it always like this?" I asked Rayna.

"Like what?" She asked, swiping her fingers across her cheeks and smearing her mascara even further.

"Such a mess."

"It's not a mess. It's organized chaos." She drifted towards a vanity. "It was there. Under the mirror," she pointed. I leaned in, heart pounding. The warning words were scrawled in garish red lipstick: "*Keep your mouth shut, or else.*" A chill shot down my spine like icy fingertips.

"Any idea who wrote it?" I snapped a picture of the note with my phone.

Rayna shook her head, but her eyes darted away, not meeting mine. I was pretty sure she was lying.

"Any model feuds or rumors floating around?"

She frowned, drifting in thought. "Nicole and I had words last week over the floral showpiece assignment. Nothing major, just typical backstage drama. But the note's message..." Rayna trailed off uneasily.

I nodded encouragingly. "Anything could be related, no matter how small or irrelevant. Take your time." She drifted in thought, piecing fragments together reluctantly. With a delicate shudder, Rayna continued. "Now that I think about it, Nicole did seem overly upset by our argument. She accused me of ... spreading stories." A subtle wave of pink washed over Rayna's cheeks before she turned away.

Voices filtered down the hall, growing nearer. I hurried across the room and snuck a peek through the cracked door.

Two officers strolled past, deep in discussion. "...

check the dumpster for anything tossed. Perp could be that sloppy." Their footsteps faded out of earshot.

Letting out a breath, I turned back to Rayna. "We'll revisit Nicole. For now, keep thinking—what do you remember?" she nodded solemnly as I pivoted, intent on inspecting the rest of the room - only to lose my balance on a stray heel.

Windmilling my arms like a demented bird, I careened towards the mirror with an "Eep!" Rayna gasped, "Look out!" but it was too late.

Bracing for impact, I tried to tuck into a roll like an action star. What ensued was more Jackie Chan bloopers reel - I bounced off furniture, crashed into the wall, and finally slammed into a clothing rack with a whoomph of expelled air.

Dazed, I wriggled out from under an avalanche of silk fabric. Rayna hovered beside me anxiously as footsteps approached. With a groan, I struggled to regain my footing. No doubt about it, I was about to get busted with a capital B. With the place crawling with cops, there was no way they hadn't heard that crash.

Sure enough, moments later, the door opened, and my heart leaped—only to sigh in relief at seeing Kade's tall frame fill the entryway.

"Fancy meeting you here," he grinned wryly,

dimples flashing. I shot him a sheepish smile from my crouched position. His gray eyes crinkled in amusement at finding me knee-deep in trouble, as usual.

"Kade! I, uh, was just…"

"What, rearranging the crime scene?" he chuckled. "You really couldn't stay away, could you?"

I gave him a sheepish grin. "You know me too well. I had to check for any clues. Considering I was here anyway, this one just fell into my lap."

Kade entered the room and held out a hand to help me up. "Some things never change with you."

Brushing myself off, I asked, "So what would you have me do?"

He placed his hands on my shoulders, expression serious. "I assume she's here, and you feel compelled to help her, that she's not going to cross over otherwise, but we're getting married in a matter of days, remember?"

"What does he mean? I'm not going to cross over?" Rayna interjected, moving to stand so close I felt the blast of her icy chill. Why were ghosts so cold?

"He means," I cast an apologetic glance at Kade, "that you're probably stuck here—as a ghost—until we solve your murder. So any clues you can shed on that front would be helpful."

"I take it she doesn't know who shot her?" Kade dropped his hands and stepped back.

"He shot me?" Rayna's screeched, the pitch hurting my ears and making me wince.

"You know who shot you?" I pounced.

"What? No!"

"But you just said he—"

"It was a general phrase," she huffed, her anger once again losing steam. "I don't know who shot me. I didn't see it happen ... I don't remember it." Her voice trailed off, but I caught the anguish in her tone.

"Memory loss isn't uncommon." I commiserated.

"Audrey," Kade warned, his deep voice holding a hint of warning. I knew where he was going with this. He knew the story. I'd be compelled to help Rayna because she couldn't help herself. "I know you want to solve this case," he began. I started to protest, but he cut me off gently. "Just listen. I'm worried you'll run yourself ragged trying to juggle it all. The last thing I want is for you to get stressed or burned out."

Reaching up, I wrapped my arms around his neck and tilted my head back. "I'll be careful, I promise. Besides, this one shouldn't take long. Shooting someone in the middle of a fashion parade? Someone had to have seen something. Between the two of us, we can have this wrapped up by the end of the day."

He grinned, sliding his hands down my back to rest on my hips. "Tell you what - you let me buy you a coffee, fill me in, and I'll see what I can do to help off the record."

CHAPTER THREE

didn't get my coffee. Kade was called away as soon as we stepped outside the dressing room. Although I lamented my lack of caffeine, I couldn't help but be pleased that it gave me some extra snooping time, for I suspected Kade fully intended to bundle me into my car and send me home as soon as we were done with coffee.

An unnerving chill raised goosebumps on my bare arms as I walked backstage. Models bundled together in anxious huddles fell silent at my approach, exchanging wary glances.

"That's her. That's Nicole." Rayna pointed.

Nicole hovered apart from the others, worrying a tissue between her white-knuckled fingers. Her watery blue eyes kept drifting to the corridor leading to the dressing room, where the police were searching for clues.

Not wanting to alarm the already on-edge group, I moved slowly, keeping my voice gentle. "Ladies, I know you're all in shock right now. I have a few questions that may help shed light on what happened."

Averting gazes or brushing tears, none volunteered to speak first. I focused on Nicole, noticing the redness creeping up her pale neck. "Nicole, could we chat privately?"

Her stricken look turned wary, though she gave a tight nod and followed me a short distance away. Hands fluttering like trapped birds, Nicole searched for words. "I-I don't know what I can tell you. Rayna and I were coworkers, that's all."

Something in her tone rang false, or perhaps it was the way blue eyes slid from mine when she spoke of Rayna. "You seem more upset than the others. Was there more to your friendship than that?" I prodded.

A visible shudder passed through Nicole's slender frame, and her thin composure nearly crumpled. "Please, I shouldn't say. It will only cause trouble if it gets out." Twisting the tissue to shreds did little to mask trembling hands.

Despite my concern for Nicole's state, I knew she held a valuable clue if only I could draw it out. Taking her clammy hands in mine, I gave them a reassuring squeeze. "I'm not the police. I'm a private investigator. Understanding Rayna's relationships may be key to finding her killer."

Seconds dragged as an internal debate raged behind Nicole's anguished eyes. At last, a single whispered word passed her lips - "Blake."

"Blake?" I probed quizzically, running through lists of names.

Nicole was breathing rapidly through her nose, chest heaving with the force of her confession. "Blake Kingston, one of the expo sponsors. He and Rayna were ... involved." Scarlet bloomed high across her cheekbones and down her neck.

The revelation took me aback. I shuffled through what I knew of Blake Kingston - a wealthy, successful businessman, devoted husband, and well-respected member of the community. Not the profile of an illicit lover. His public persona stood at odds with what Nicole was accusing him of.

Breaking the stunned silence, Nicole blurted, "Please don't judge her. She cared about him so much. Rayna thought it was true love that he'd leave his wife for her someday. But I warned her not to trust such empty promises..." Her speech dissolved into hitching breaths as Nicole fought back tears.

I gave her hands another gentle squeeze. "Nicole, I need you to tell me everything you know about Blake and Rayna's relationship."

She searched my face pleadingly as if hoping for a reprieve. But Nicole knew as well as I that this secret carried weight in solving the case. Steeling herself with a long inhale, she unraveled the threads of Rayna's tragic affair.

The story spilled out in fits and starts, a jumbled chronology of passionate encounters and simmering jealousy. Behind closed doors and away from his family, Blake doted on Rayna with luxurious gifts and whispered promises. But Nicole recounted the tension growing as divorce rumors threatened Blake's public image.

My mind raced, connecting dots. Blake Kingston, a dashing figure of success and sophistication, married to the elegant and loving Olivia, was once the epitome of a perfect couple. Only the façade of marital bliss has cracks beneath the surface. Blake's eyes had wandered, leading him into the arms of Rayna Mills, a stunning and ambitious model. What started as mere fascination turned into a torrid affair, a dangerous liaison that threatened to unravel everything Blake had built. With his affair with Rayna a ticking time bomb, the fallout could not only destroy his marriage but tarnish his reputation forever.

An argument the night before. Was it over breaking things off or taking the relationship further? Both motives rang true as possibilities.

Nicole wound down, colorless and shaky. Beyond shocked by the hidden double life, new pieces of the puzzle snapped into place. I had my first solid suspect and means for murder.

Rayna stood next to me throughout the whole damning story. Her translucent features registered a torrent of emotions - sorrow, regret, embarrassment. Colorless lips parted as she whispered, "Is this really how my secret came to light? Through Nicole?"

I spoke under my breath. "Her telling me may help catch your killer." Rayna seemed unconvinced, glancing at Nicole's turned back nervously.

Reaching out uselessly, she pleaded, "Please don't think ill of me, Audrey. I know affairs are wrong, but Blake made me feel so alive. I never meant for things to escalate this far." Tears welled and streamed down her pale cheeks.

My heart went out to her, even in death,

ashamed yet yearning for understanding. "Rayna, all that matters now is the truth."

She sniffled, bowing her head. "I just wish..." Her spirit faltered, choked by regret for roads not taken. Reaching instinctively, my hand passed through her shoulder consolingly.

In that fleeting contact, I felt an impression of Rayna's longing - for passion fulfilled, loose ends untied, goodbyes unsaid. A life cut cruelly short with futures now forfeit, consequences left for others to shoulder. All that remained was one last act of justice for her silenced voice; for whatever sins Rayna had committed, she surely didn't deserve this.

Thanking Nicole, I moved away, jerking my head for Rayna to follow.

"It really would have helped if you'd told me this yourself," I hissed. "You know when I was asking you earlier if anyone wished you harm?"

"What?" Rayna blinked her electric blue eyes. I noticed she'd taken a moment to fix her makeup, the smeared mascara removed to reveal her original dramatic makeup. Was that a ghost thing? I'd never really noticed it with ghosts before. Maybe it was a model thing, for Emily's makeup was always immaculate, and I'm sure she'd shed a tear or two since her demise.

"That you're having an affair! Did his wife know? Nicole says there was an argument. What was it about?"

Rayna stiffened, lifted her chin, and then fanned her cheeks. "You firing all these questions isn't helping!" She spun on her heel and stormed off, back rigid. Before I could follow, a commotion from the front of the stage caught my attention.

"What do you mean, it's evidence?" A woman's raised voice reached my ears. "I need to see if it can be repaired. Salvaged. Do you have any idea how much that dress is worth?"

"I'm sorry, ma'am, I really am," Kade soothed. "I wish I could return the dress to you, but as I've already said, it is evidence."

"But that stain needs to be treated now! If you let the blood dry, it's going to stain permanently."

"In case you didn't notice," Kade's words held a trace of steel, "there's also a bullet hole in the bodice. The blood stain surrounding it will not make that much difference."

"Says you," the woman muttered.

Reaching the corner of the stage, I remained in the shadows and watched. Kade looked down, his eyes meeting those of the woman standing before him. Though she was notably shorter than him, she carried an air of confidence that seemed to level the playing field. Her platinum blonde pixie cut framed her face, giving her a youthful, edgy vibe. Oversized, fashionable glasses perched on her nose, accentuating her green eyes. While she wasn't the waifish figure of the models backstage, her slightly fuller physique emanated a genuine warmth, like someone who enjoyed life's small pleasures without reservation.

"Heard a whisper on the ghost vine that the fashion show got derailed," Ben drawled in my ear. I'd felt a chill brush over me a millisecond before he appeared, warning me one of my ghosts was about to make their presence felt. I was so relieved it was Ben I wanted to hug him.

"There you are," I smiled, genuinely pleased to see him. "I could use your help."

"What you got?" Ben watched as paramedics eased Rayna's body from atop the giant cake. Crime scene tape was already strung around the perimeter, and the once-teeming hall now stood empty. Vendor stalls were abandoned partly due to panic and partly due to the police shutting the expo down.

"Rayna Mills, model, shot." I jerked my head toward Rayna's body. "Her ghost is about here somewhere."

"I'll go find her in a second. What else?"

"Note left in the dressing room, warning her to keep her mouth shut. Written in lipstick. And she was having an affair with Blake Kingston."

Ben whistled. "Juicy."

I grinned. "Right. I mean, motive for murder? Absolutely."

"Didn't I see his name on a poster around here?"

I nodded. "He's a sponsor." Which, as far as I was concerned, made him my number one suspect. Did he sponsor the expo purely to get his mistress a modeling gig?

"Who's the blonde?" Ben looked over my shoulder to where Kade was taking down the woman's information.

"I think she may be the designer?" I chewed my lip, head cocked, as I tried to recall her name. Seb had mentioned it earlier before everything had turned to chaos. "She's asking for the dress back."

"Ha! Fat chance," Ben scoffed. "Why would she even want it? It's ruined."

"Agreed, but there's a lot of probably very expensive fabric that isn't ruined—I mean, the skirt part of the dress has yards and yards of fabric that she could potentially reuse. And I have to confess, the gold color is simply stunning." My eyes darted across the stage where Kade was engrossed in something the dress designer had said. "I can't shake the feeling that—"

Before I could finish the sentence, my phone blared to life in my hand. The screen flashed "Mom" against a photo of her smiling face.

"Mom," I answered on the second ring, keeping my voice hushed. While I wasn't exactly hiding, I didn't want to draw attention to myself either, less Kade—or anyone else for that matter—had me removed from the crime scene.

Too late, Kade had spotted me, looking in my direction, eyebrows raised, and I gave him an apologetic shrug.

"Audrey, where are you?" Mom's panicked voice came down the line. "You said you were going to get your purse, and that was ages ago. They won't let us back in. What's happening in there?"

Crap. I'd forgotten the lie I'd told my family. Of course, they were waiting for me outside, worried out of their minds when I didn't show up.

"Sorry, Mom, everything is fine," I soothed. "I'm fine. It's just... there's been a murder."

Mom was silent. Then Laura's voice was in my ear. "Don't tell me. You're helping the police with the investigation?"

"Am I on speaker?" I dodged the question.

"You're getting married in two days," Amanda chimed in. "Now is not the time to get embroiled in something like this. Leave it to the experts."

I was definitely on speaker. "Seb, can you take everyone home, please? The expo is over, canceled, and please don't wait around for me. I don't know how long I'll be."

"Will do," Seb replied. "Don't forget, we have an appointment at the spa at nine tomorrow morning."

"I still don't see the point," I whined. I'd been waxed, plucked, tweezed, and fake-tanned to within an inch of my life. Another spa appointment was the last thing I wanted or needed.

"This one is pure relaxation, girlfriend," Seb assured me. "A little girly fun before the big day. You're going to love it. There's a floatation tank."

"Whatever that is," I grumbled.

"We'll see you tomorrow," Mom was back. "And Audrey? Please be careful."

"Always am, Mom."

CHAPTER FOUR

"I thought you'd left?" Kade, having finished with the blonde, joined me and Ben.

"Nope." I glanced over his shoulder, watching the woman hurry away in the opposite direction. "Who was that?"

"That was designer Marianne Thompson."

"Ah! I knew I knew it." I declared.

"Knew what?"

"Her name. Seb mentioned it earlier, but I couldn't remember it. So that's Marianne, huh? And she wants the dress? Is that usual?"

Kade shrugged. "For clothing that the victim was wearing? Yes. But we're often asked to return evidence we've collected at a crime scene, be it a phone, jewelry, or something like that."

"Is she a suspect?"

Kade shot me an unfathomable look and crossed his arms over his chest. Okay. Message received. Butt out of his investigation. "Although you said you'd help off the record." I reminded him.

I watched him trying to fight off a smile, his lips twitching almost imperceptibly as he pressed them together.

"At this stage, everyone's a suspect," he relented. "Although at first glance, I see no motive. She potentially had the opportunity as she had access backstage, knew the routine, and therefore knew that the confetti cannon firing would effectively mask the gunshot." That explained the odd sound I'd heard when the confetti cannon had gone off. I'd heard Rayna being murdered.

"Right," I nodded, looking to where the shot was fired. I pointed toward the rafters, where an officer dusted the railing for prints. "You think the shooter was up there?"

"The ME can confirm trajectory, but we believe the bullet came from above rather than below stage level."

"Your turn," Kade prompted. "If you want me to share intel, then turnabout is fair play."

He had a point. Plus, as competitive as I was, this was one case I wanted solved sooner rather than later, and if that meant pooling resources, I was all for it.

"So the victim, Rayna, has been having an illicit affair with Blake Kingston," I told him. "One of the other models, Nicole, told me." I glanced around, making sure no one else was in earshot. "Rayna confirmed."

"Is that right?" Kade's brows shot up, and he rocked back on his heels.

"You'd have seen the note in the dressing room?" I continued. "Warning Rayna to keep her mouth shut?"

Kade frowned. "You think that was Kingston?"

I barked out a laugh. "Hardly his style," I scoffed. "It was written in lipstick. Ninety-nine percent sure a woman wrote that note."

"One of the other models," Kade stated. "Any idea who?"

"All I know is that Rayna disagreed with Nicole last week. Rayna said it was about a flower arrangement or something, but I think it was about the affair. But that doesn't make sense for Nicole to leave the note. She was genuinely distraught at what's happened to Rayna."

"Detective!" Officer Sarah Jacobs called from backstage. "They've found something in the dumpster out back."

Kade kissed me hard, his lips meeting mine in a desperation that surprised me. Then he broke away abruptly and spun on his heel, joining Officer Jacobs with purposeful strides.

"Want me to check it out?" Ben asked, dragging my mind away from its preoccupation with Kade's butt, where my eyes lingered.

"Actually, yes." I dragged my eyes away to focus on Ben. "I'm going to find Rayna."

Ben followed Kade while I ducked backstage, pausing where the models were gathered, searching for Rayna. Not finding her with the others, I hurried down the hallway to the dressing room. Slipping inside undetected, I spied her sitting at her makeup station, now covered in fingerprint powder.

"What do you know about Marianne Thompson?" I asked, crossing to the rack of dresses I'd knocked down earlier and began picking them up.

"The designer?" Rayna paused, dusting nonexistent powder across her flawless skin, and swiveled to look at me. "Not much. Why?"

I shrugged. "No reason, just curious. She was keen to have the dress you were wearing returned to her, but the police are keeping it as evidence."

"It's a beautiful dress," she sighed, resuming dusting the brush across her cheekbones. Of course, neither the makeup nor the brush was corporeal, but there was no need to tell Rayna that. She'd had an eventful day as it was.

"Gold is a somewhat bold choice for a wedding dress." I'd almost finished picking up the rack full of dresses, puffing from the exertion—they were heavier than they looked when Rayna cocked her head and said, "Someone's coming."

I froze behind the clothing rack, hidden by the row of bulging gowns, peeking between the dresses as the dressing room door opened and a man walked in. He wasn't toweringly tall—maybe about 5'9"—but he carried himself with a confidence that filled the room. His slim, fit build spoke of someone who took care of himself but wasn't obsessed with the gym. His shaggy, brown hair gave him a roguish look as if he often ran his fingers through it, leaving it in artful disarray.

"Oh God, it's Leo Simmons," Rayna groaned,

tossing her makeup brush on the dresser and glaring at the man.

I opened my mouth to ask who Leo Simmons was but closed it, not wanting to give away my hiding spot. Instead, I watched as Leo's eyes scanned the room before heading toward Rayna's station. Did he know it was hers, or was it just a lucky guess?

But he vetoed the dresser with the makeup scattered across it to focus on the floor beneath instead. He was crouched on one knee, patting across the dusty floorboards with one hand while muttering, "Where is it?" when the door slammed open, and whom I could only presume was another model stormed in, fury emanating from her, her glare landing squarely on Leo.

"You've got no business being here!" She practically vibrated with rage, her cheeks flushed, her eyes flashing. The heightened emotion only added to her beauty, but I figured she didn't need to know that—what woman wants to hear she looks pretty when she's mad?

Leo straightened to his full height and rolled his eyes. "Clara. What do you want?"

"I know you're writing a story about me, Leo," she cried. "You're going to ruin my career."

Leo laughed. "You? Honey, do you honestly think I care?"

Clara tucked a strand of hair behind her ear and frowned. "What?"

"You might be the center of your universe, but you're a mere blip in mine. I'm writing about something far more important."

Clara's eyes shot to Rayna's dressing table. "You're writing about Rayna." She sounded oddly defeated. "Her death is a tragedy—"

Leo interrupted. "A tragedy that sells. Unlike your cliché struggles."

"So, you're not writing about me?"

Leo rolled his eyes. "Writing about you would be a waste of ink."

The look of relief on Clara's face was impossible to miss, but neither was the disgust. "I can't tell if I should be grateful or offended."

Leo smirked and said, "Save your emotions; you'll need them for the runway. Now, if you'll excuse me, I have a story to break."

"You're a parasite," Clara snapped, stalking out of the room.

"Careful, sweetheart," Leo called after her. "All this attention might make me curious as to *why* you don't want me to write about you!"

"Hey!" Officer Noah Walsh appeared in the doorway. "What are you doing in here? The dressing room is off limits."

Officer Walsh scanned the room, didn't spot me behind the dress rack, thank God, then grabbed Leo by the arm and escorted him out, berating him the entire way. "I don't know why journalists think they are above the law," Officer Walsh said as they made their way out of earshot, "but a crime scene is off limits—press included."

After I was sure they had gone, I crept from my hiding spot and quietly shut the door.

"Leo Simmons is a jerk," I said to Rayna, who'd returned to her makeup, apparently disinterested in the little display I'd just witnessed.

"He's a cockroach," she agreed.

"Why would Clara think he was writing about her?"

Rayna shrugged. "Clara has an eating disorder to go with her self-esteem issues. She thinks people are talking about her—it—all the time."

"And are they? Talking about her?"

Rayna snorted. "Only if she brings it up. Honestly, none of us care. We're in this gig for our own careers. Today was my big break. Top model wearing a Marianne Thompson design. I'd get national coverage, possibly international attention. Instead..." she stood and began pacing. "Instead, someone *killed* me, and now I'm... this!" She waved a hand toward her incorporeal body. "So excuse me if I'm not that sympathetic towards Clara's worries if Leo Bloody Simmons is writing a story about her."

"You're missing the point."

"Oh, please!" Her eyes narrowed, and the corner of her mouth curled ever so slightly, but it spoke volumes. Her sneer is so nuanced and calculated that it shifts the surrounding atmosphere. Feeling another tantrum imminent, I quickly continued before she could gather steam.

"Let's just say, for argument's sake," I held up a finger to shush Rayna when she would have interrupted. To my eternal relief, she shut her mouth and let me finish. "That Leo was writing a piece about Clara and her eating disorder. Something she was desperate not to get out. Obviously, Clara isn't going to tell Leo about her disorder herself, is she? No. So he'd ask other models to talk to him and dish the dirt. And you said it yourself: you're all in this for your own careers. So if throwing Clara under the bus would eliminate a small portion of the competition... you'd do it, wouldn't you?"

"I wouldn't." Rayna protested. "But I see your point. There are certainly other models who would."

"So if Clara is paranoid like you pointed out, then having Leo sniffing around is bound to upset her. To fuel her belief that he's about to expose her secret. Which would explain why she came barging in here shaking with rage."

Rayna froze, her eyes widening as she stared at me. "Oh my God," she breathed, "you think *Clara* left the note?"

"Do you think she'd do something like that?" I countered. "Regardless, we have no proof, just a theory."

"I know how we can prove it," Rayna said, sounding smug. "You know how I said Clara has self-esteem issues? Yeah, well, to help with that, she writes affirmations on her mirror."

"Ah," I snapped my fingers and grinned. "You're thinking we can compare her handwriting to the note? I like it. Which dresser is hers?"

Rayna led me to a dresser tucked away in the corner, and sure enough, scrawled on the mirror with red lipstick were the words, "You are more than your reflection."

Opening my phone, I pulled up the photo I'd

taken of the note, then held it up to compare. "Looks to be the same shade of lipstick. And look, the handwriting is the same."

Rayna's eyes widened, and her perfectly sculpted eyebrows shot up toward her hairline, framing her eyes in surprise. Her full lips, usually set in a confident smile or a knowing smirk, parted ever so slightly, a small gasp escaping between them.

"It *was* Clara." For a moment, her immaculate poise shattered. "Do you think she... *killed me*?"

I shook my head. "I don't see how. She was with the others who rushed onto the stage to help you. There wasn't enough time for her to pull the trigger and get down to the stage. No, I think all that Clara is guilty of is leaving you the note." Plus, murdering Rayna would not stop Leo from writing the story Clara thought he was writing. No, I was reasonably sure if Clara was going to commit murder to stop Leo's exposé, it was Leo she'd kill.

Rayna's usually elegant posture sagged as she slumped to the floor, the golden gown flouncing around her, catching the light and sparkling in its ethereal beauty.

"Are you okay?" I'd thought Rayna would be pleased. We were making progress.

"I'd thought for sure that whoever left that note was the killer." She admitted. "But you're right; it couldn't have been Clara. Even in all the chaos, I remember seeing her crying at the base of the cake. She didn't kill me."

"No." I was confused. "I thought you'd be pleased."

"You don't understand..." she whispered, tugging at the lace of her gown.

"Explain it to me," I urged.

"Earlier, you said a woman wrote the note—because of the lipstick. And now we know it was Clara. And for reasons that didn't have anything to do with me. So all this time, I'd been thinking that Blake..." she choked, and her eyes welled with tears. "That Blake..." she tried again, but her throat closed, and she couldn't get the words out.

"You thought the killer was a woman. Therefore, it couldn't have been Blake?"

She nodded, tears breaking free as she took in a shuddering breath. Her transparent figure glowed faintly in the dim light, a heavy weight of emotion emanating from her. Empathy surged within me; she was in love with a potentially lethal catch—a married man who might also be her killer. As her gaze wandered, searching the void for answers, I could almost sense the inner turmoil wrestling within her. She was a ghost caught in the worst kind of purgatory, where love morphed into potential betrayal.

"What's that?" She pointed, and I followed her gaze. There, on the floor, a few feet from Rayna's dresser, was a book, half hidden beneath an article of clothing.

Picking it up, I turned it over in my hands. The notebook was far from pristine, bearing the marks and scuffs from constant use. Its black, leather-like cover was worn at the edges. The elastic band meant to keep it closed had lost some elasticity over time, barely clinging to its function. Inside, the pages were a mix of chaos and order, a battlefield of ink where some sentences were carefully written while others seemed to be captured in a frantic hurry.

Sticky notes peeked out from various pages, color-coded in a system that only made sense to the user. Symbols, abbreviations, and shorthand notations populated the margins, each a secret language I couldn't decipher.

"This is what Leo was looking for," I said. Rayna picked herself off the floor and joined me.

"Oh yeah, that's his all right. I've seen him writing in it."

"You have?"

"Oh yeah," she nodded. "Leo Simmons has been stalking me for weeks."

CHAPTER FIVE

"*Y*ou don't think that's something you might have mentioned earlier?"

"Don't use that sassy tone with me," she scolded, back ramrod straight. "I hardly think it's relevant that a *reporter* has been following me. It's his job, after all."

"Did it not occur to you that maybe he was following you to catch you and Blake together? That he wasn't putting together a story about *you*, but rather he was getting ready to expose Blake's adultery to the world?"

"You make it sound so tawdry," she whined.

"Rayna, look," I held up the notebook and pointed. On the page, Leo had scribbled Blake's name. "Leo knew, or at least suspected, that the two of you were involved."

"Yes, well, it doesn't matter. Blake was taking care of it."

I felt a sharp pang of disbelief cut through me. "Blake was taking care of it?" I repeated, just to be sure I'd heard her right. "Are you saying Blake *knew* a reporter was tailing you?"

"Why has your face gone red?"

"Rayna!" I snapped. I knew my face had gone red. I could feel the heat in my cheeks burning so hot I was surprised my skin wasn't on fire.

"Okay, fine, that was what Blake and I argued about the other night. I told him about Leo, but honestly, I thought Leo was writing a piece about me."

"I bet Blake didn't think that, though, did he?"

"No, he did not," she grumbled. "He turned a similar shade of red."

My hands involuntarily clenched into fists, crumpling the pages of the well-worn notebook. "You're telling me this now?" I said, struggling to keep my voice steady. My eyes met hers, and for a moment, I saw a flicker of regret cross her features. But the moment was brief, and my frustration did not abate. Here I was, invested in solving her murder, and she'd been holding out on me. For the first time, I questioned the trustworthiness of my ghostly client.

Just as I'm grappling with this new turn of events, Ben comes strolling through the dressing room wall.

"Wow, the tension here is thicker than my mom's Sunday gravy," he said, a touch of concern rippling across his face. "What's happened?"

I let out a half-hearted chuckle, relieved by Ben's presence but still jarred by Rayna's revelation. "We're just rearranging the puzzle," I said. "Pretty sure it was Clara, another model, who left the note for Rayna." I quickly filled him in on what had transpired, including Rayna holding out that Blake Kingston had known his affair with Rayna was about to make front-page news. He was already my number one suspect, and now he was my top number one it-couldn't-possibly-be-anyone-else suspect.

"Rayna," Ben clicked his tongue in disappointment. "You gotta be straight up with us. We're here to help, but we can only do that if you tell us everything. And I mean everything."

"It wasn't Blake!" She protested vehemently.

"And what if it was?" I said. "Do you really want to protect a murderer?"

"He wouldn't. He loved me. He was leaving her. Go ahead, ask him yourself."

"Oh, I intend to," I assured her, but I was talking to thin air; Rayna had disappeared. I turned to Ben. "Gah! She is so frustrating."

He gave a half smile and slapped me on the back, his icy palm connecting with my lungs and sending me into a coughing fit. "You might need to cut her some slack, Fitz. She's been dead all of five minutes."

Catching my breath, I admitted he was right. Just because I was on a time crunch and wanted to solve Rayna's case so I could skip off happily into the sunset and get married didn't mean I couldn't give her some consideration. The poor girl hadn't had the chance to come to terms with the idea that the person who killed her was not only someone she knew but highly likely it was someone she loved.

"So," I wheezed, rubbing my knuckles against the center of my chest to generate some warmth. "What did they find in the dumpster?"

"Smith & Wesson Model 642 Airweight snub-nosed revolver. Most likely the murder weapon once the medical examiner confirms the bullet that killed Rayna was a 38."

"So the killer shoots Rayna, then chucks the gun in the dumpster on their way out."

"Or—," Ben began, but I cut him off. "Or?"

"Or," he repeated, folding his arms, "the killer tossed the gun, then came back here, hiding in plain sight."

"My theory fits if Blake Kingston is the killer."

"And if he isn't?"

I didn't like Ben's question, so I ignored it. Leaving the backstage area, I returned to the row of seats in front of the runway. It hadn't all been a lie. I *did* leave my bag behind. Spotting it beneath one of the fold-up chairs, I scooped it up, shoved Leo's notebook inside, and tossed the strap over my shoulder.

Kade's deep and smooth voice carried a teasing tone as he asked, "Leaving so soon?" His hand slid around my waist, effortlessly pulling me against him. I leaned back into him, drawing comfort from his warmth and strength.

"I could hang around if you need my help," I teased back, gazing up at him.

"The trouble is, babe, your help is more of a distraction." Kade's lips quirked in amusement, and I grinned.

"Awww." Spinning around to face him, I kissed

his lips softly. "Fear not, detective, I am departing." I winked playfully before taking a step back.

Kade raised a brow. "Really? You're actually leaving?"

His skeptical look made me laugh. "I have a suspect to question. Oh, that reminds me, that threatening note left for Rayna? You'll want to talk to Clara about that."

"Clara?"

"One of the other models." I waved vaguely at the stage. "It was more of a misunderstanding than anything. Clara mistakenly believed that journalist Leo Simmons was writing a story about her eating disorder and was interviewing Rayna to get the inside gossip. The note was warning her to keep her mouth shut."

"Who *was* he writing about?"

"Rayna thinks he was writing about her. I think he was preparing to blow the lid on her affair with Blake Kingston."

Kade rocked back on his heels. "Wait a second," he said, holding his arms out as if to stop me. His eyebrows dipped low over his gray eyes, and he pursed his lips together in a thin line. I knew that expression. He was working through the case with me, wondering which direction my thoughts were taking him. I stopped and sighed, standing up straighter myself. "So you're off to question..." He paused. "The journalist?" he added hopefully, but I could tell from his voice that he already knew it was a trick question.

I grinned. "Nope. My number one suspect, Blake Kingston," which elicited a scowl from Kade.

I gave a little wave as I walked away.

"See you tonight. Be careful!" He called after me.

I marveled at the house as Ben and I drove up the winding gravel drive to the Kingston mansion. It was grand, the kind of place that screamed 'old money' rather than nouveau riche. Ivy crawled up the stone walls, and large windows gave a peek into the opulence that lay within.

"Wow," I muttered, half to myself and half to Ben. "Just look at what money can buy."

The path ended in a grand circular driveway. A fountain graced the center of the loop, water glistening as it leaped from the mouth of a stone cherub. Parking my SUV, I felt like a fish out of water.

Taking a deep breath, I stepped out of the car,

smoothed my T-shirt, resisted the urge to check for stains because, for sure, by this time of the day, I was bound to have spilled something on myself, and made my way to the oversized front door framed by two pristine hedges. I raised my hand to ring the doorbell, half-expecting a butler or a maid to answer.

The door swung open, and there, in a stunningly gorgeous dress that probably cost more than a small car, stood Olivia Kingston. Aside from my surprise that she'd answered the door—I was expecting a staff member—my breath was temporarily stolen by Olivia herself. Her beauty was timeless, a blend of classic charm and subtle allure. Her eyes, a soft shade of green, revealed a compassionate and understanding spirit. Framing her face are gentle waves of chestnut hair that fall effortlessly, reflecting her innate grace.

Everything that I'd ever heard about her was true. Olivia Kingston was grace personified, gliding through life with poise and elegance. Why on earth would Blake have an affair with Rayna Mills when he had Olivia waiting at home for him?

"Yes?" she asked when I stood there with my mouth open. "Can I help you?"

I cleared my throat. "Sorry. Yes. I'm here to see Blake."

She arched a delicate brow. "Do you have an appointment?"

"I do not. But I think it's in his best interest to speak to me." I pulled out a business card, slightly dogeared, and held it out. "I'm a private investigator here on behalf of my client, Rayna Mills, recently deceased."

Olivia's back stiffened, and the soft smile froze on her face. Her eyes moved from the business card I held out to my face. "Who?"

Ben let out a hoot and pointed at her. "That's a lie! She knows exactly who Rayna Mills is." Despite his sudden outburst making me jump, I agreed with him. Although subtle, Olivia's demeanor turned icy at the mention of Rayna's name.

Before I could answer, she plucked the business card from my hand and studied it. "Recently deceased, you say? What happened?"

"Rayna Mills was murdered this afternoon at the bridal expo."

"Ah," Olivia nodded. "Blake was a major sponsor of the expo. I assume you're speaking with everyone involved."

"Interesting how she is completely avoiding

mentioning Rayna. Not even surprised there's been a murder," Ben said. I agreed with his observation.

"Is Blake here?" I prompted.

"No, he isn't available. He went to the barn. It caught fire."

I frowned. "Isn't your barn in the backyard?"

"No," she said. "The barn is located several miles away on a different property."

"So, not here?" I asked, dumbfounded. How much land did these people have that they had an entire barn on another property?

Olivia chuckled lightly, her laughter sounding pleasant to the ears. "That's what we call it. We bought an old and dilapidated barn a few years ago and fixed it into an event space for weddings, parties, corporate gatherings, etc."

A heavy feeling of dread settled over me. "It isn't The Harvest Moon, is it?" *Please say it isn't, please say it isn't*, I prayed silently. The Harvest Moon was where Kade and I were getting married.

"Why yes, it is! You've heard of it?" She seemed delighted, and my heart fell into my shoes.

"My fiancée and I are getting married there in two days."

"Oh. Oh my dear, I'm so sorry," she reached out and patted my arm consolingly. "From what I understand, the fire was quite extensive. An electrical fault, I believe. Blake has gone down to see for himself and arrange for the insurance assessor."

"When—" my voice came out as a high-pitched squeak, and I had to stop and clear my throat before continuing. "When did this happen?"

"Lunchtime today. I'm so sorry to be the bearer of bad news. I'm sure someone will contact you to let you know what is going on. Blake and I don't manage the day-to-day running of the barn. We leave that to the manager. But, you know, maybe it isn't that bad, and your wedding can go ahead as planned." She didn't believe that any more than I did.

"Thanks for your time," I said, keeping my voice steady despite the blow. Walking back to my car, I tried to collect my thoughts.

"That's really tough timing, Audrey," Ben said softly as I slid behind the wheel.

"Yeah, it is," I murmured. I was torn. Part of me knew I should drop everything and start the hunt for a new venue. But then there was Rayna, her face appearing in my mind's eye. Could I put her justice on hold?

The two obligations sat in front of me like weights on a scale. My thoughts drifted to Kade, our families, and the commitment we were about to make. But they also veered towards Rayna, who'd get none of those things and whose murderer still walked free.

"Wow, talk about a dilemma," Ben noted, echoing my thoughts.

"You said it," I agreed, feeling the weight of both responsibilities. "But you know what? The wedding is a celebration, and it'll happen one way or another. Justice for Rayna, though—that's a one-time opportunity."

"So, we're sticking with the investigation?" Ben asked.

"We are. But first, let me make some calls. We need to find a new venue, that's all."

Pulling away from Chalet Kingston, I hit Seb's number on speed dial.

"Tell me you're on your way back," Seb answered on the first ring.

"I hope you're sitting down. The venue for the wedding is toast. Literally," I sighed. "An electrical fire."

"I just got a call from Karen from the Harvest Moon. There's been a fire. She says they'll be closed for repairs for at least a month," Seb said simultaneously.

"I know," I sighed.

"Did they call you too?"

"No. I'm at the Kingston's house looking for Blake, and his wife said he's at The Harvest Moon due to the fire."

"They say they'll do their best to find us an alternate venue," Seb was trying to sound cheerful for my sake, but I could hear the doubt underlying his words.

"It'll be fine," I lied, trying to be optimistic.

"Of course it will," he lied back. "Are you coming home?" he asked hopefully.

I chewed my lip. Despite having given Rayna's murder precedence, the guilt was intense. "I just have a couple of things to take care of," I hedged. "Can you manage without me for a little while longer? Maybe Mom and Laura can make some calls to help with the venue situation?"

"One hundred percent," Seb assured me. "Your time is better spent helping solve a murder, especially if that means one less ghost crashing your wedding." He was aware of Emily's sporadic appearances and Ben's continuous presence, but he didn't want me to deal with Rayna as well when I walked down the aisle, assuming there was an aisle for me to walk down.

CHAPTER SIX

I pulled up to The Harvest Moon, my heart pounding. The last time I was here, Kade and I discussed wedding table placements. Now, the thought of table placements seemed like a cruel joke.

The air was tinged with the acrid smell of burned wood and melted plastic. The scent clung to my nostrils, mixing uneasily with the lingering aroma of the leaves that carpeted the ground.

Fire trucks were parked haphazardly on the lawn, their lights still flickering but sirens silent. Firefighters were conversing with a visibly stressed man I presumed to be the fire chief. It seemed they had things under control, but the shell of the venue told a different story. Charred beams protruded like skeletal ribs from the main hall. The floor-to-ceiling windows that once showcased the idyllic countryside were shattered, and what remained of the curtains dangled in tatters.

Seated on a foldable chair near one of the fire trucks was Blake. His face was drawn and weary. He was jotting down notes on his tablet, presumably already calculating the cost of repairs and the insurance claims.

My eyes met his for a fleeting second. There was a lot I wanted to say and questions I needed to ask. The fact that my dream wedding venue had turned into a disaster zone was devastating, but the fire had also cast new shadows on Blake—shadows I couldn't ignore.

"Are you okay?" he finally called out as he got up, his voice tinged with a concern I wasn't sure was genuine.

My lips parted, but no words came out. Was I okay? Far from it. My dream wedding was in ashes, literally. And my number one suspect in Rayna's murder? He was standing right in front of me, the glow from the still-smoking ruins illuminating the conflicted man that was Blake Kingston.

"I need to talk to you about Rayna," I said,

breaking the silence. My voice was firm; my eyes locked onto his.

"Rayna?" He looked at me with feigned ignorance, brows slightly arched. "I can't say that name rings a bell."

"Don't play games, Blake. Rayna Mills," I emphasized, watching his reaction closely.

For a second, his façade slipped. His eyes widened slightly, and I knew I had hit the mark. Then, as quickly as it had come, the moment of vulnerability was gone, replaced by his usual self-assured composure.

"I know a lot of people. You'll have to be more specific."

"She was shot. Killed," I blurted out.

Blake froze. Whatever mask he had been wearing shattered in that moment. His tablet slipped from his grasp, landing soundlessly on the grass below. His face drained of color, and he swayed as if his legs could no longer hold him.

"What?" His voice was barely a whisper, thick with disbelief. "Rayna's dead?"

"Yes, she's dead. Murdered. And I know you and she were... involved."

Blake staggered back as if I had physically pushed him. "This can't be," he mumbled, running a hand through his perfectly styled hair. "I—We weren't—"

His hesitation spoke volumes. He was floundering, struggling to maintain the charismatic demeanor that had won over many people. The silence stretched between us, thick and uncomfortable.

"I need to know what happened, Blake. If you're innocent, now's the time to prove it," I said, my voice tinged with suspicion and skepticism. "Because right now, you're my number one suspect."

Blake looked utterly devastated, starkly contrasting to the suave businessman the world knew. But before I could entertain any sympathy, my thoughts returned to Rayna—cold and alone on a morgue table.

"I can't believe Rayna is gone," he murmured. "But you need to understand. I had nothing to do with this."

"Then you won't mind answering some questions?" I pushed. "We can start with why Leo Simmons was tailing Rayna."

His eyes shot up, widening with a mixture of surprise and dread. "Leo Simmons, the journalist? What does he have to do with this?" His lie hung heavy in the air.

"He was following Rayna before she died," I replied, watching his reaction closely. "He was investigating something. Something that might have led to her murder."

Blake's jaw clamped shut, and his hands balled into fists at his sides.

"I don't know anything about that," he said through gritted teeth. "But I can tell you one thing. I loved Rayna. And I would never have hurt her."

"Then why were you lying to me?" I asked, not letting up. "Why did you pretend not to know her when I first brought her up?"

Blake sighed heavily, shaking his head. "I didn't want to get involved in any of this," he admitted. "When you brought up her name, it caught me off guard. I didn't know how to react."

"So you pretended not to know her?" I pressed.

"I didn't want to draw any attention to myself," Blake said, his voice low and tight. "If people learned about our relationship, it would have opened up a whole can of worms."

"Well, the police will want to talk to you," I said, my tone cool and detached.

"You're not the police?" he said cautiously.

"I'm a private investigator," I revealed, locking eyes with him. "I specialize in solving mysteries, you could say. And right now, you're smack dab in the middle of one."

He blinked, absorbing the information, then looked me over as if seeing me for the first time.

"I must admit, you don't look like any private investigator I've ever met," he said, his voice tinged with a curiosity that made me uncomfortable. "What's your name?"

"Audrey Fitzgerald," I said, watching his reaction closely. "And for the record, you don't look like any murderer I've ever met, either. But appearances can be deceiving, can't they?"

Blake's body tensed, and his eyes drifted to the charred remains of The Harvest Moon.

"You're right," he said, his voice barely audible. "Appearances can indeed be deceiving."

A firefighter in a soot-streaked jacket approached Blake. "Mr. Kingston, could I have a word? We've got some preliminary findings you'll want to hear."

Blake shot me a look. "Excuse me, Audrey. This won't take long."

While Blake was busy conferring with the firefighter, Ben floated toward me, his expression thoughtful. "I've been poking around inside. If this was arson, it's professionally done. No obvious accelerants or funky burn patterns, but the timing sure is convenient, huh?"

I nodded, contemplating the implications. "Blake seems genuinely surprised about Rayna's death. But it could all be an act."

"I've seen better actors, and I've seen worse," Ben mused.

Blake returned a couple of minutes later, looking somewhat perturbed. "Sorry for the interruption," he said. "This fire has created complications for everyone."

"No worries," I replied, keeping my tone neutral. "I've got more questions for you, though. Where were you when Rayna was killed?"

"Which was?"

"Just before two-thirty this afternoon."

"In a business meeting," he said, his voice steady. "A high-stakes meeting via video conference. It ran long, or else I would've been at the expo. The meeting had just wrapped up when I got the call about the fire. I came straight here."

His answer felt rehearsed, setting off warning bells in my head. A video conference could easily be faked.

"Do you own a gun, Blake?" I pressed on.

He hesitated before nodding. "Yes, I do. For

protection, of course. My lifestyle demands certain security measures."

I glanced at Ben, who shook his head subtly. Something wasn't adding up, and we both knew it.

"I'll need to speak with you again," I told Blake, looking him squarely in the eye. "We're not done. Not by a long shot."

"Sure," Blake said, matching my gaze. "As I said, I'm not going anywhere."

I nodded, pushing a stray lock of hair away from my face as I contemplated my next steps. Blake Kingston was a puzzle wrapped in an enigma, hidden behind a confident façade. And every new piece of information only seemed to complicate the picture.

As I turned away, Blake suddenly spoke up. "I hope the fire hasn't put too much of a dampener on your wedding plans. Finding a new venue on such short notice must be difficult."

I stopped in my tracks, startled by his words. I hadn't told him that. Had he been talking with Olivia? My eyes narrowed. "You seem quite concerned for someone who has his own problems to deal with."

"Can't a man multitask?" Blake smiled, but the warmth didn't reach his eyes.

Ben floated closer, almost as if he were guarding me. "I don't like this, Fitz. The guy's slippery as an eel."

"Tell me about it," I whispered back, thankful for Ben's comfort, even if no one else could see him.

As I returned to my car, my thoughts were a swirl of confusion and suspicion. Blake had given me answers, but each one only led to more questions. And as Ben had pointed out, the timing of everything—the fire, Rayna's murder, the destruction of my wedding venue—was just too convenient to be a coincidence.

As I slid into the driver's seat, my phone buzzed with a new message. It was from Seb: *Emergency meeting. Call me ASAP.*

Taking a deep breath, I started the engine and pulled away from The Harvest Moon, my eyes glancing at the rearview mirror one last time. Blake was still standing there, watching me, and I couldn't shake the feeling that my dealings with him were far from over.

As I opened my front door, the first thing that caught my eye was the sparkle of my wedding dress. It hung gracefully on the stairway railing, almost like a celestial being that had descended into my living room. Mom was beside it, needle and thread in hand, carefully sewing a delicate piece of lace into the lining.

"Mom, you've taken the dress out," I said, my voice tinged with surprise and caution.

She looked up, her eyes crinkling at the corners as she smiled. "Ah, you caught me! I couldn't resist. I'm adding the finishing touches—your grandmother's lace and a vintage button from my wedding dress."

Mom had chosen the spot to hang the dress well; the late afternoon sun streamed through the window, casting a warm glow on the beaded floral lace and shimmering tulle.

"It's perfect," I said softly, touched by her sentimentality.

Mom placed her needle on the small table beside her and stood up. "This is more than just a piece of fabric, Audrey. It's a rite of passage, and I want you to feel our family's love and history with you as you walk down the aisle."

I nodded, feeling a lump form in my throat. "Thank you, Mom. I'll cherish it."

She hugged me warmly and then looked at the

dress, her expression pensive. "I hope you'll have an aisle to walk down, Audrey."

I blew out a breath. "Me too, Mom."

Bandit and Thor stirred from where they'd been napping on the sofa, catching the last rays of the late afternoon sun.

"Mom!" Bandit screeched at the top of her lungs. "You're home!"

"Cor, easy there," Thor winced, rubbing a paw over his ears. "Some of us aren't deaf."

"Sorry, Thor, sorry, Mom," Bandit leaped off the sofa and ran to me, little legs stretching up my thigh, eager for pats. I obliged.

"Hey, Bandit," I crooned, scratching the raccoon behind the ears. "What have you been up to today?"

"We've been watching Mom make your wedding dress!" she declared, and I couldn't help the laugh that escaped. I'd hardly call Mom sewing in the keepsakes as making the dress, but Bandit was easily impressed, and her heart was always in the right place.

Thor jumped from the sofa and slowly stretched. "Good. Now that you're back, you can feed me. Your Mom refused, saying nonsense about being told she's not allowed to give me any treats. And Seb ran out of here like his tail was on fire. Something about an emergency. You know what the real emergency is?" He trotted over to his bowl, half full of kibble. "This!" He eyeballed the bowl dramatically. "How am I expected to survive on this?"

"Thor," I chuckled, leaning down to pick him up and cuddle him to my chest, burying my face in his soft, thick fur. "You are not starving, and you most definitely are not wasting away. You're so dramatic."

"I have to say," Mom said behind me, "that the two of them are most chatty. It was a pleasant reprieve when they fell asleep."

"Hey," Thor protested, wriggling to be put down, his tail twitching with annoyance. I lowered him to the floor, whispering, "She didn't mean to be rude."

He didn't believe me, for the glare he shot my mom could have cut through steel. Mom laughed. "Goodness, would you look at that look he's giving me? It's almost like he can understand us."

"I think animals understand more than what we think," I said as diplomatically as possible.

Bandit's nose twitched, her eyes following movement outside the glass door. "Mom, it's Seb!"

Thor lifted his head from his paws. "Ah, Seb. Maybe he brings food as a tribute."

The door slid open, and there stood Seb, my friend, neighbor, and an increasingly indispensable wedding planner. "Audrey, thank God you're home. I heard your car."

I walked over to greet him with a hug. "Hey, Seb. Thor was lamenting your earlier disappearance. Something about an 'emergency'?"

Seb chuckled, but there was a serious glint in his eyes. "Well, given the Harvest Moon situation, you could say things have been... fiery."

I sighed. "You have no idea. Come in."

As Seb stepped inside, Thor and Bandit trotted up to him as if he were their long-lost uncle. Seb reached down to give them both a few loving pats. "Hello, my furred constituents. Keeping the realm safe?"

Thor purred, a tacit seal of approval, while Bandit danced at Seb's feet.

Seb straightened up and took a deep breath. "Audrey, I've called every venue in town. Everything's booked. But don't worry, I have a plan. A last-ditch plan, but a plan."

Mom, who'd been quietly observing, chimed in. "At this point, any plan that doesn't involve the fire department is a good plan."

Seb's eyes met mine. "Trust me, Audrey. I've got this. You focus on walking down that aisle, wherever it may be, and leave the rest to me."

I looked from Seb to my mom, then at the dress hanging from the railing, glowing in the soft indoor light. The burdens of the day seemed a little less heavy.

"It's okay, Seb. I trust you. If you say you've got this, then you've got this."

Seb nodded, a determined smile forming on his face. "You bet I do."

CHAPTER SEVEN

*K*ade pushed open the front door, balancing a bag of groceries in one hand and his phone in the other. I waited for him to cross the threshold, the lines of worry on my face slipping away as he approached.

"Hey," he said softly, enveloping me in a warm embrace. "What happened?"

My chest constricted, anxiety creeping into my bones. "The wedding venue burned down. Every alternative is booked, but Seb says he has a last-ditch plan."

Kade wrapped me up tighter in his arms and kissed my forehead. "There must be another option that we haven't thought of yet; just give Seb a chance to think about it. He isn't messing around when he says he can take care of things, Audrey. You know that better than anyone."

I nodded and took a deep breath, trying to catch hold of my erratic emotions. Kade was right: if Seb said he had a plan, it would happen without any hiccups—and I couldn't believe how much that comforted me.

My eyes met his, and I found comfort in the steadiness of his gaze. "Yeah, I know."

Kade glanced from my face to Mom and Seb's, who had been chatting animatedly about the wedding decorations. His gaze returned to me as he asked, "Do you think we might need some alone time?"

"Yes," I said with feeling.

He thanked them for their help before he escorted them to the door. "Audrey and I just need a few minutes on our own," Kade politely clarified, and understanding seemed to pass between them. Without argument, they departed.

Once they were gone, Kade went to the kitchen, pulling ingredients from the bags. "How does a simple pasta sound? Something light and easy?"

"Perfect," I said, relieved not to have to think about any decisions, even ones as simple as dinner.

As Kade cooked, the aroma of garlic and basil

filled the air. He set the dining table with candles, transforming the space into our own intimate restaurant. Once everything was ready, he pulled out a chair for me, ever the gentleman.

"There's something oddly romantic about discussing a murder case over a candlelit dinner," Kade said, breaking the silence.

I chuckled. "Only you could make that sound appealing."

He leaned in, his eyes serious. "If there's one thing I know that will make you happy, it's solving a crime. I know you've been beating yourself up you haven't been able to solve Emily's murder. But I also know how amazing you are, and I have full faith that you'll catch the killer."

"Thank you for believing in me," I whispered, touched by his unwavering support.

"Thank you for being the love of my life," Kade added. "So, let's review Rayna's case and the suspect list. Who had the most to gain from her death?"

"Top of the list is Blake Kingston."

Kade looked intrigued. "He certainly has a motive."

"It makes sense, though," I argued. "Blake's career, his reputation, his marriage—all could be ruined if his affair with Rayna came to light. He's got the most to lose."

Kade forked a piece of pasta thoughtfully. "But what does he gain from her death? Because even with Rayna out of the way, that story could still run."

"Would it, though? Blake's a rich man. Lots of resources are available to him. Probably be easy for him to get the story squashed with the lead witness dead."

"But if that were true, surely he could get the story squashed without killing Rayna. Not to mention one tiny detail. He wasn't at the expo."

"It's entirely possible he sneaked in and out with no one noticing. I wouldn't put it past him." I countered, leaning forward.

Kade chuckled. "Audrey, that's bordering on implausible. The expo was full of people. Security was tight."

"You know as well as I do that people can find a way if they're motivated enough," I said, stubbornly holding onto my theory. "Besides, Blake has resources. If anyone could bypass security measures, it's him."

Kade looked at me before breaking into a smile. "You are remarkable, you know that? Your mind works in ways that never cease to amaze me."

I felt a blush creep up my cheeks. "I just want to find the truth."

He reached across the table, taking my hand in his. "And we will, Audrey. We'll unravel this mystery step by step. If Blake's our man, we'll find the evidence to prove it."

"If?"

Kade's eyes narrowed thoughtfully. "Have you considered Olivia?"

"Olivia?" My eyebrows shot up in surprise. "Blake's wife?"

He nodded. "Exactly. What if she knew about the affair and wanted to stop Rayna from ruining her marriage? Olivia also has a lot to lose if this all comes out into the open."

I thought for a moment, the wheels in my mind turning. Olivia had always struck me as a strong, resilient woman who prized her marriage and the life she'd built with Blake. The thought of her as a suspect hadn't seriously crossed my mind. Until now.

Kade continued. "I did some digging. Olivia was at the expo earlier in the day. She left before the fashion parade started, which could be because she didn't want to see Rayna."

"Hmm," I mused, swirling the last bit of my wine

around the glass. "You're saying she had both motive and opportunity?"

"Exactly. Now, I'm not saying she did it, but shouldn't you at least consider her a suspect?"

I leaned back, thinking it over. Ignoring a potential lead because it seemed improbable was a rookie mistake I couldn't afford to make.

"You make a valid point," I conceded, setting my wineglass down. "Olivia had motive, and she was at the scene earlier. She 'could' be a suspect."

Kade squeezed my hand, a twinkle in his eyes. "Let's sleep on it."

"Kade Galloway, why do I sense sleeping is the last thing you have in mind?" I teased, batting my lashes.

"I don't know," he winked, standing and pulling me to my feet, "why do you think that?" He placed a soft kiss on my lips. I kissed him back, feeling the heat between us intensify. As we pulled away, I glimpsed something primal and possessive in his gaze that made my heart race.

"What if we solved the case tonight?" Kade murmured against my lips. My pulse quickened as excitement thrummed through me. "How?"

Kade leaned back, his eyes sparkling with

mischief. "We follow the evidence until we find the killer."

"And then?" I asked, playing along.

"And then we celebrate."

A cacophony of shrill laughter, shouts, and what sounded like applause yanked me out of my sleep. My eyes snapped open, and I stared at the ceiling, momentarily disoriented. Was I dreaming?

I glanced at my alarm clock—3:07 a.m. This was no dream. With a loud groan, I forced myself out of bed, stumbling towards the source of the noise. As I made my way downstairs, I mentally prepared myself for whatever bizarre spectacle awaited me.

I was not disappointed.

Bursting into the living room, I found Emily and Rayna sashaying around like they were on a fashion runway, complete with exaggerated turns and poses. Ben sat on the armrest of my couch, whooping and hollering like a teenager at a rock concert.

"Work it, ladies, work it!" Ben cheered, his ethereal form glowing with excitement.

Emily threw an air kiss his way before flipping

her hair dramatically while Rayna twirled in a circle, her laugh filling the room.

"Strut your stuff! Make the room your runway!" Bandit cheered from her seat on the coffee table, her eyes darting back and forth as she followed the action.

"Ha! You call that a turn? I've seen dumpsters with more grace!" Thor was less impressed. He lounged on the kitchen counter, throwing occasional snarky remarks.

"Are you all completely mad?" I finally burst out, half annoyed and half entertained.

Emily and Rayna stopped mid-pose, looking like guilty children caught with their hands in the cookie jar.

"Oh, Audrey! You're up!" Emily chirped. "We were just having a bit of a fashion face-off. It's important to stay in practice, even in the afterlife. You know how Lumina Models is; they drill us to hit our marks and make every pose count."

Rayna's eyes widened. "Wait, you're with Lumina? I'm with them too! No wonder you've got the moves down."

"Small afterworld," Emily giggled. "How about joining our fashion show, Audrey? Practice before the big day," Emily invited.

As I looked at the eager faces before me—both living and dead—I felt the weight of their unsolved murders, yet I also felt a warmth, a sense of camaraderie that was hard to explain.

"All right," I conceded, kicking off my slippers. "Move over. Show me how to work this ghostly runway."

After the impromptu imaginary fashion show, the energy in the room was infectious. However, the weight of two unsolved murders still loomed over me. "All right, guys, as much as I'd love to continue being a supermodel, there are cases to solve," I declared, reluctantly pulling away from the fun.

Rayna and Emily exchanged understanding glances before vanishing, leaving me with Ben. Thor and Bandit had already tapped out, snoring their heads off on the sofa.

Too tired to sleep, I retreated to my home office. The whiteboard on the wall was a chaotic sprawl of scribbled notes. Watching Emily and Rayna together tonight had brought something into focus that I hadn't considered before.

Standing in front of the board, my eyes skimmed over the facts and questions. Two models. Two bridal gowns. Two murders. As my gaze landed on the word "Lumina Models," written in my own hurried handwriting, it hit me like a bolt of lightning.

What if their cases were connected? It just seemed too much of a coincidence that the two models, both murdered while wearing stunning bridal gowns, had no link. Granted, their deaths were a year apart, and Emily's case had gone cold. But what if the reason Emily's spirit had been hanging around, unavenged and restless, was because she and Rayna shared the same killer?

The room felt suddenly electric, every nerve in my body buzzing with the intensity of this newfound connection. I felt like I was standing on the edge of a breakthrough, and the thought excited me.

Picking up a marker, I drew a bold line on the whiteboard connecting Emily and Rayna's names, linking them to Lumina Models. It was a tenuous link, yes, but sometimes a single, fragile thread is all you need to unravel a whole tapestry of deception.

Turning away from the whiteboard, I sank into my chair and booted up my computer. It was time to delve into Emily and Rayna's lives; I had a fresh lead to follow, and I couldn't afford to waste a minute.

Slowly, my eyes grew heavy, the words on the screen blurring into a jumbled mess. Before I knew it, my head drooped onto the desk, my last thought being that I was on the cusp of something crucial.

———

The scent of coffee wafted through the air, dragging me out of my slumber. My eyes flickered open, and I found myself face-planted on my desk, a puddle of drool sticking a sheet of paper to my cheek.

"You're going to need this," Kade said softly, setting down a cup of freshly brewed coffee next to me.

I lifted my head, the paper glued to my face. "What time is it?" I mumbled, still half-asleep.

"Time for you to get ready for your spa day. Remember? You've got an appointment, and you're running late," Kade reminded me, leaning down to give me a gentle kiss.

The spa day—completely forgotten amidst the chaos of solving two murders. Sighing, I looked at my disheveled state in the reflection of my computer screen. "I look like a wreck." Plucking the paper from my cheek, I ran my hands over my face, scrubbing away the last vestiges of sleep.

"You look like a beautiful wreck who's working too hard," Kade said, pulling me up from the chair.

"Go. Relax. Everything will still be here when you get back."

"All right, all right, I'll go," I said, a tinge of reluctance in my voice. "I promised Seb, after all."

Kade looked puzzled. "You don't sound too excited. Isn't a spa day supposed to be fun?"

"Last time I had a spa day, they wrapped me in seaweed that smelled like a sewage treatment plant. It's hard to find inner peace when you're gagging on the stench." I grimaced at the memory.

Kade chuckled. "Well, maybe this time you can skip the fragrant oceanic embrace and just go for a massage or something."

"Sounds like a plan," I nodded, draining the last of my coffee. Despite my reservations, the prospect of a spa date was growing on me.

After quickly changing, running my hands through my hair, and giving my teeth a cursory brush, I made it to the spa only ten minutes late, huffing and puffing as I swung the door open.

"You're late," Amanda announced, her eyes checking the designer watch on her wrist.

"I had a parade to attend," I quipped, sliding my sunglasses up to perch on top of my head. "A very exclusive midnight fashion show."

Mom rolled her eyes. "You and your colorful imagination, Audrey. You should write a book."

"If only you knew, Mom," I muttered under my breath.

Seb stood up, his eyes sparkling. "Ladies, if you're ready, I have reserved something extra special for us today. Something that will wash away all your stress."

Mom beamed. "That sounds divine, Seb. What is it?"

"A float tank experience," he announced proudly. I vaguely recalled he mentioned something along those lines earlier, but I hadn't been paying close attention.

"A float... what?" My eyes widened. "You're not wrapping me in stinky seaweed again, are you?"

"No, no," Seb laughed. "This is different, I promise. Think of it like meditating in water."

"I didn't bring a swimsuit," I countered, looking for an escape route.

Laura waved a piece of fabric in the air triumphantly. "Thought ahead. Brought you one."

"Rats," I sighed. "Okay, but wouldn't a massage be simpler?"

Amanda gave me a stern look. "Audrey, Seb went through all this trouble to plan something special for you. The least you could do is to be grateful and try it."

I hated it when Amanda was right. Cornered, I relented. "Fine, let's do this float thing."

The tank lid clicked into place, plunging me into an all-encompassing darkness that seemed to stretch on forever. A profound silence filled the space, muffling the outside world until all that remained was the subtle swish of water cradling my floating body. Muscles I didn't even know were tense relaxed, untangling the web of stress that had formed from juggling a murder case and a wedding disaster. On the cusp of sleep, I felt my worries dissolve into the warm water.

That's when a sudden sound shattered the tranquility. Adrenaline surged through me, kicking my limbs into a frantic dance. In that moment of disorientation, I forgot where I was and what was happening. My arm flung out wildly, and I whacked my forehead against the tank's side.

Wincing from the impact, I let out a startled fart, sending a small flurry of bubbles frothing around me.

I burst into giggles, laughing at my own involuntary spa upgrade. "Who needs bath bombs when you've got natural talents?" I said to myself, rubbing the spot on my forehead that was already throbbing.

It dawned on me then—the float tank was soundproof. Which meant whatever I'd heard had come from inside. "Ben. Why am I not surprised?"

His laughter echoed in the confined space. "You got me. Sorry, I couldn't resist."

I couldn't help but chuckle, even as I touched the tender spot on my forehead. "I know you, Ben Delaney, and you're not sorry at all."

"Audrey, are you okay?" the spa attendant called, lifting the lid to check on me.

"Yeah," I stammered, blushing. "I, uh, fell asleep and woke up confused."

The attendant nodded, lowering the lid again.

"Was there a reason for the interruption, or are you just here for the laughs?" I asked, squinting into the darkness.

He chuckled. "No reason, just curious what a float tank was like. Well, I guess I'll leave you in peace."

"Wait," I hissed, wriggling to face him, water

sloshing over my legs. "While I was dozing, I had a thought."

"About?"

"You can read electronic data, right? Go check Blake's computer for any trace of that supposed video call meeting. There has to be a digital footprint if he was really on it."

"Consider it done," Ben whispered, then nothing but a silence so loud I could hear it.

"Ben?" I whispered. No reply. Figuring he'd gone, I settled back in the tank, but this time, sleep was elusive, my thoughts consumed with Rayna's murder.

CHAPTER EIGHT

*T*he hinges of the front door creaked softly as I stepped inside, glad to be home. Despite my initial reluctance, I'd actually had a lovely morning at the spa. After the float tank, I'd had a sublime massage that had reinvigorated yet relaxed at the same time. I definitely felt better for both, but now it was back to reality.

There it was—my wedding dress. Hung carefully on the banister of the staircase, it commanded attention, its silk and lace fabric reflecting a soft glow from the late morning sun filtering through the living room window.

"I can't believe I'm getting married tomorrow," I whispered, my fingertips grazing the delicate lace. Of course, I didn't know *where* I was getting married.

We'd been unable to secure a new venue, but Seb assured me he had it under control and the wedding would go ahead.

"There you are," Ben said, appearing beside me. "You know how Blake was your number one suspect? Bad news; he's clear. The digital recording proves he was on a video call at the time of Rayna's murder."

Rayna was hot on Ben's heels. "See! I told you Blake wouldn't harm a fly."

I crossed my arms, skepticism furrowing my brows. "Rayna, walk me through the argument with Blake. Do you think his wife, Olivia, knew about the affair?"

Rayna's elation dissipated. Her ghostly features drooped. "I don't know. Our last big argument wasn't even about us, really. It was about Leo and his stupid exposé."

"Yeah, I get that, but I need you to think back, to remember. Was Blake upset, specifically, about his wife finding out? Or more that his reputation was about to be dragged through the mud?"

"Both, I think. Though he didn't specifically say, he was worried about Olivia finding out. Just that she was going to kill him."

I sighed, rubbing my temples. "That shoots Olivia right up on my suspect list."

Rayna nodded, her gaze meeting mine. "It's getting complicated, isn't it?"

"It was never simple," I replied, glancing one last time at my dress before grabbing my keys. "I need to talk to Blake again," I declared, heading for the door. "Find out what Olivia knew."

"He's at his office," Ben called after me as I headed out the front door. "While you do that, I'm going to check out this Leo Simmons guy."

Blake's office building had the comfortable familiarity of small-town professionalism—air that was crisp but not too sterile, mingled with the subtle aroma of freshly brewed coffee and copier ink. Navigating through the hallways adorned with framed local artwork, my shoes squeaked on the laminate flooring. Eventually, I arrived at a simple wooden door with a burnished plaque that read "Blake Harrison, CEO." Across the hall, Blake's assistant caught my eye from her workstation; she gestured for me to go on in. Taking a moment to gather my thoughts, I knocked softly on the door and waited.

A voice yelled, "Come in," and I pushed the door open.

"Audrey," Blake greeted, his voice polished but laced with a calculation that made my skin prickle. "Do come in. I've been expecting to hear from you. This week has been, shall we say, taxing?"

I stepped into his office, its spaciousness accentuated by the minimalistic furniture. A large, clutter-free desk sat in the center, framed by expansive windows that offered a sprawling view of the town below. He gestured for me to sit in one of the sleek leather chairs opposite his desk.

"I have news that is both good and less-than-ideal," I began, keeping my eyes on his as I sat. "You're off my suspect list for Rayna's murder. Your alibi checks out."

His shoulders relaxed just a fraction, a seasoned gambler not showing his full hand. "Well, that's a relief."

"But," I interjected, locking eyes with him, "let's talk about the elephant in the room. Does Olivia know about your affair with Rayna?"

The corners of his eyes tightened, and he paused as if considering multiple angles before committing to an answer. "No, she doesn't. And I would prefer it stay that way."

His eyes locked onto mine, their depths veiled, offering no clue to his thoughts. It was as if he was silently bargaining and subtly warning me all at once. The atmosphere in the room turned electric with tension.

"Secrets tend to surface," I cautioned. "Especially when lives are involved."

"I'll cross that bridge when I come to it," Blake said, his voice tinged with a cold acceptance.

After a moment of silence, dense with unspoken understanding, I changed gears. "Rayna thought you were going to leave Olivia for her. Was she just a plaything, or was she something more?"

Blake stiffened. He turned his back to me, his eyes fixed on the window overlooking Firefly Bay. The shimmering waters glinted in the sun.

"It's complicated," he finally replied, his voice loaded with a subtext I couldn't quite decode.

"You were living a double life," I summed up, unable to keep a touch of bitterness out of my voice. "Caught between two worlds, loyal to neither."

His eyes locked back onto mine, their depths swirling with an emotion I couldn't place—remorse, perhaps, or maybe it was just the fear of being exposed.

"Exactly. And now the consequences of those choices are catching up, aren't they?" He nodded, but it was a nod that gave nothing away, a skill he had probably mastered over years in the boardroom.

For a moment, we both sat in silence, absorbing what he'd just said. It felt like we were both realizing how complicated love and relationships could be. With Rayna gone, Leo's exposé hadn't simply vanished; if anything, her death infused it with a darker, more salacious element that could catapult his career to new heights. I stood, preparing to leave, catching the resigned slump in Blake's shoulders from the corner of my eye. It became painfully clear he knew it, too.

I sent Blake a last look of acknowledgment before exiting his office. I emerged into the bright sunshine and made my way to my car, my mind drifting to more pressing matters.

Next stop: Olivia Kingston. Something told me it was going to be a conversation worth having.

I found myself back at the Kingston estate, pulling my car into the familiar parking spot from just a day ago. I reached for the doorbell, hesitating briefly, wondering what sort of reception I'd receive today.

When the door swung open, Olivia stood there, a picture of timeless elegance in a simple yet form-fitting dress. Her chestnut hair framed her face in gentle waves. Did she have a stylist on retainer just to look this perfect every day?

"Audrey, back again so soon. To what do I owe this visit?" she said, her voice guarded.

"Would you be free to talk?" I asked.

"Of course," she responded, stepping aside to let me in.

Inside the light-filled foyer, classical music played softly, mingling with the distinct scent of freshly brewed tea. I accepted a cup but didn't sit.

"I heard you were at the bridal expo but left before the fashion show," I began, sipping my tea, wishing it were coffee. She met my gaze with an inscrutable look.

"Commitments are a never-ending cycle, aren't they?" she replied, avoiding my implied question.

"I have to ask, Olivia—did you think Blake was having an affair?" I waited, watching her closely as she hesitated.

"There are many kinds of affairs, Audrey. Not all of them are romantic," she said, her voice measured, her gaze finally breaking to look down at her own cup.

That's when Rayna appeared near the piano. "Wow, she's good. Makes you work for every crumb."

Startled, I almost spilled my tea. "Sorry, a little shaky today," I said, putting the cup back onto its saucer.

Olivia gave me an unreadable look. "If you say so."

"Where were you at the time of Rayna's death, around two-thirty yesterday afternoon?" I pushed on.

"I was doing charity work, meeting with others in the organization to plan our next fundraiser." She answered.

"Would there be anyone who can vouch for your whereabouts?" I pressed, annoyed she was being vague with the details.

"Of course. I'll have my assistant send you an email with the particulars," Olivia assured me.

Rayna rolled her eyes at me. "Talk about stonewalling."

"Thank you. One more thing, if you don't mind," I said cautiously. "Blake mentioned owning a gun when we spoke earlier. May I see it?"

Olivia looked at me, her brows knitting together. "Isn't that more of a job for the police?"

I met her gaze squarely. "I'm working in coordination with them on this case." It wasn't entirely a lie. Kade and I were working together, even if it was unofficial.

"In that case," Olivia said, seeming satisfied. "I suppose that would be okay."

We walked into the den, a cozy room awash in warm, earthy tones. Deep mahogany bookshelves lined the walls, filled with an eclectic mix of literature and artful trinkets. Olivia crossed the room to an imposing oil painting that hung on the wall in a gilded frame. The portrait captured both her and Blake in happier times, smiling at the world and each other as if they were the only ones in it. She reached up and gently swung the painting forward on hidden hinges, revealing a wall safe tucked cleverly behind it.

Making sure her back blocked my view, Olivia entered the combination. The safe emitted a soft beep, and the heavy metal door swung open. Her eyes scanned the safe's interior, and I watched as her poised expression faltered for just a second.

"That's odd. The gun—it's missing."

Rayna chuckled softly. "Well, aren't you the actress? Almost had me fooled."

Olivia's face paled, her eyes widening. "This isn't good. I had no idea it was missing."

"Who else has access to the safe?" I asked, pulling out my phone.

"Blake, of course. Maybe the housekeeper, but she's been with us for years. Blake's head of security, Jeff, perhaps," Olivia stammered, her composure slipping.

"What sort of gun was it?"

She shrugged. "I don't know. I don't like guns; I've never gone near it. It stayed in the house under one condition—it had to be locked in the safe."

I dialed Kade's number, moving toward a secluded corner of the room where an ornate antique desk sat—far enough that Olivia wouldn't overhear me but close enough that I could keep an eye on her.

"We have an issue, Kade," I whispered urgently into the phone. "Olivia Kingston isn't giving anything away. But what's more concerning is that Blake's gun is missing from their safe. You need to bring her in for questioning."

Kade's voice carried a tone of deep concern. "Are you okay? This sounds serious."

"I'm fine, but we're losing time here. The missing gun from the safe might be the same one found in the dumpster, the one that killed Rayna. You have the resources and forensic expertise to confirm."

"Dare I ask how you even know about the gun we found in the dumpster?"

I coughed, clearing my throat. Oops. "Uh, Ben may have mentioned something."

I could practically hear him shaking his head. "Figured as much. Anything else I need to know?"

"Just that Ben checked Blake's alibi, where he said he was on a video call. It checks out."

"Good to know, but I can't put that in a police report," Kade drawled. "Not that I'm casting aspersions on Ben, but did he check thoroughly that the recording hadn't been tampered with in any way? I know date and time stamps can be manipulated. We need to send that data to the forensics team so that they can officially rule Blake out."

"Is it wrong that I'm kinda pleased he's still on your suspect list?"

"You really think he's behind this, huh?"

A breath of frustration slipped out. "I want him to be. I'm worried I may be unintentionally forcing this investigation to point at Blake." My voice dropped to a conspiratorial hush. "Or Olivia."

"I'll bring them both in. We need to work quickly if we want to wrap this up before our wedding tomorrow."

"Exactly. I'll meet you back at the station. Love you."

"Love you too. Stay safe," Kade replied, and I hung up, tucking my phone back into my purse.

Turning back to Olivia, who was now gracefully rearranging some books on a shelf, I said, "Thank you for your time, Olivia. I'll get out of your hair. Please expect a call from the police for further questioning."

Her eyes narrowed ever so slightly, but her smile never wavered. "Of course, Audrey. One must do what one must."

As I left the Kingston estate, Rayna rode shotgun, singing a Taylor Swift song about heartbreak so off-key my ears hurt. I couldn't wait for us to solve her murder and usher her on to the afterlife.

CHAPTER NINE

*a*s I walked into Kade's office, he looked up and smiled. "You know, you've got this whole 'serious but smokin' PI look going on. Makes me want to frisk you for contraband."

I grinned. "Really? Because you've got that 'charming detective who breaks all the rules but still gets results' vibe. What's for lunch? Day-old donuts and stale coffee?"

He chuckled and pulled out a couple of sandwiches from a paper bag to go with the fresh cups of coffee in takeout cups sitting on his desk. "Ah, the classics never die. But for you? Only the best."

Pulling up a chair, I grabbed a coffee and took a grateful gulp. I really wasn't a tea drinker, but I'd accepted the beverage Olivia had offered merely to be polite.

"So?" I asked, snagging a sandwich. "Did I beat them here?"

"Of course you did. I've only just sent a patrol car out to pick 'em up."

"Good, that gives us time to go over the case."

"I knew you were going to say that." Kade swiveled his chair towards the computer. "Feast your eyes on this cinematic masterpiece."

I leaned forward, almost sliding off the edge of my seat as I watched the grainy CCTV footage play. It was of Olivia at the expo, having an intense conversation with an unidentified woman. Whatever was said had clearly shaken her.

"Wow," I said, "she looks like she just found out her favorite soap got canceled mid-season. Do you think she just found out about her husband's affair? Who's the other woman?"

"No clue," Kade replied, "but she's now on my list of 'People to Question Before I Say I Do'."

I laughed. "Let's make sure that list is empty by tomorrow. Speaking of questions, any news on that gun?"

"Still waiting on forensics. But the missing gun from the Kingston's safe *could* be the same one we found in the dumpster," he said, serious for a moment.

"The same gun that killed Rayna," I mused aloud. "That would put Olivia and Blake right in the hot seat."

Kade looked at me. "We're really doing this, huh? Solving a murder the day before our wedding?"

I met his gaze. "Well, it's not traditional, but neither are we."

Kade took another bite of his sandwich, savoring it, before looking up at me. "You won't believe what else we found near the crime scene, caught on the stairs leading up to the rafters."

I raised an eyebrow, taking a sip of my coffee. "Let me guess, another false lead?"

He chuckled. "Not quite, although you're not far off. More like a red thread—to be precise, a tattered bit of cloth that matches Olivia's dress from the expo."

I nearly choked on my coffee. "You're kidding. That's almost too convenient."

Kade grinned. "Right? So, I'm getting a search warrant to look through Olivia's wardrobe for any, ahem, fashion faux pas that might match our little scrap of evidence."

I laughed. "Oh, you're really *tailoring* this investigation to meet all kinds of needs, aren't you?"

Kade pointed at me, chuckling. "Ah, a pun. You're definitely the one for me."

I smiled back, the weight of the case momentarily lifted. "Well, let's just say if you can't make a pun during a murder investigation, when can you?"

Our eyes met, and for a split second, the gravity of what we were dealing with—the serious nature of life, death, love, and commitment—pulled us closer.

Kade cleared his throat. "So, once the warrant comes through, you in for some high-stakes, high-heel investigation?"

I grinned. "Absolutely. Sans the heels. And only if I get to be the bad cop. I've always wanted to interrogate a wardrobe."

He laughed. "Deal. Just to be clear, though, you'll still be walking down the aisle with me tomorrow, right?"

I turned towards him, and our eyes met in a silent promise that despite everything going on, I was his without question.

"Wouldn't miss it for anything," I said quietly, clinking my cup to his in an unspoken agreement.

Just as we lowered our coffee cups, Kade's phone

buzzed loudly on his desk. He glanced at the screen and frowned. "Ah, it's work. I've got to take this."

I nodded, picking up my sandwich again. "Go ahead. Duty calls."

As he answered the call, his face changed, morphing into his professional detective persona. "Galloway. Yep... understood, I'll be right there."

He hung up. "Olivia and Blake just arrived."

My heart skipped a beat. "Well, things are moving quickly."

Kade got up and grabbed his jacket. "I have to go, but will you be okay here for a bit? You can use my office."

I smiled, "Of course."

As he left, I couldn't shake the feeling that we were on the brink of something, a revelation that would crack the case wide open. That, or this sandwich was giving me indigestion.

I opened my bag and pulled out my laptop to review the notes I'd taken. There were still too many pieces missing from the puzzle and too many questions unanswered. I wasn't sure how to solve any of it by the time Kade came back into the room. He looked serious, holding an evidence bag. He carefully set it on the table and stared at me until I gave him my full attention. "What?"

My pulse quickened as he pulled out a garment that looked like it had come straight from Olivia's closet. The elegant dress was unmistakably the one she wore at the expo. "Is that...?"

Kade nodded. "Seized from her home. It should contain all kinds of valuable evidence if we can find something. But look here." He pointed to the hem and seams and raised his eyebrows in question. No sign of tearing or damage.

I exhaled a sigh. "So, the fabric at the crime scene wasn't from her dress."

He shook his head. "Doesn't seem like it. And the altercation Olivia had at the expo? She claimed it was with a stranger who targeted her for being 'wealthy and elite.'"

I arched an eyebrow. "Really? A random social justice warrior at a bridal expo? Sounds like the set-up for a bad joke."

"Or a convenient lie," Kade mused. "Anyway, she said she didn't know who the woman was. Something doesn't add up."

I stared at the dress, pondering the tangled web Olivia was weaving. "That doesn't make her innocent, but it also doesn't make our job any easier."

Kade sighed, folding the dress back into the

evidence bag. "I'm going to have forensics compare this fabric with what we found anyway, just to cover all bases."

"Good idea," I said. "No harm in double-checking."

Just then, my laptop pinged with a new email. Opening my laptop, I scanned the message on my screen. "Ben's sending through something." I opened the attachment. "He's pulled more security footage from the expo, including what happened in other areas of the town hall."

Kade looked over my shoulder. "Ben is definitely a handy asset to have. What are we looking at?"

I scrubbed through the footage until I found something interesting. "Here," I pointed to the screen. "That's Leo Simmons, the journalist I told you about. He's writing an exposé on Blake and Rayna."

Kade squinted at the screen. "Time-stamp puts him far away from the stage when the murder happened. That's an alibi."

"Yes, it is," I said, feeling a mix of relief and frustration. "But the fact that he was at the expo still makes him a person of interest. I want to talk to him. With his knack for digging up dirt, he might know something we don't."

"Remember to be careful."

"Always. So, what now with Olivia and Blake?"

"Running down Olivia's alibi. It looks like Blake is in the clear, but I'm still having his alibi collaborated by those in attendance, just in case the video recording was tampered with. His gun is missing—he claims his security guy, Jeff, took it for a maintenance check. We're trying to track him down to confirm the gun's whereabouts."

I nodded. "Sounds like a plan. And I'll set up a meeting with Leo. Hopefully, he can shed some light on this."

Kade had just stepped out of the room when I reached for my phone. My eyes ran over the names in my contacts, looking for Leo's number. Rayna Mills was a case we had in common. She was my afterlife client, and Leo had been gathering intel on her for his exposé. I hoped he could be an ally. Punching in his digits, I was eager to find out what he knew.

I sat there, my finger hovering over the call button. Should I wait for Ben to tell me what he'd discovered or just dial now? Eventually, I decided to press it, listening to the rings and feeling my shoulder tense up with anticipation.

"Simmons," a voice finally answered.

"Leo, my name is Audrey. We haven't met, but we're both interested in the Rayna Mills case. I think it's time we pool our resources."

It took a few seconds for him to respond. "Audrey, is it? I'll bite. Seaview café, one hour?"

"Sounds good," I said cautiously. "But let's be clear: this is off the record until we decide otherwise."

"Fair enough," Leo replied, a note of intrigue coloring his voice. "I'll see you then."

After I hung up the phone, I grabbed my laptop and wrote a quick goodbye note to Kade. Then I took off to the Kingston estate to see if I could find their security guard before his officers did. Blake had a reputation for being slippery, so I had a hunch he might have thrown them off. When I arrived at the circular driveway, I parked and headed over to the staff entrance that I'd noticed the last time I was there and mentally filed it away under 'useful places to make a sneaky entrance.'

Jeff, Blake's head of security, answered my knock. His brows lifted in surprise at seeing me. "Haven't seen you around here. What can I do for you?"

"I was hoping to ask you a few questions if you have a minute?"

He hesitated but then nodded and gestured for

me to follow him to his office, a small nook tucked away from the foyer. "What can I do for you?"

I cut right to the chase. "The police told me Blake's gun is missing. He said you took it for maintenance. Can you tell me more about that?"

Jeff's body tensed, almost unnoticeably, but I saw it. His unease was a chink in the armor.

"Yes, standard procedure. Thought it best after..." He trailed off.

"After what?" I prompted.

His eyes met mine. "After that journalist started snooping around, asking questions."

I fixed him with a look. "And?"

Jeff exhaled slowly. "Between you and me? I had a bad feeling. Call it instinct, but something didn't sit right about the situation."

His unease surprised me and stirred my own suspicions in kind. "Thanks for being upfront. I might swing by again for more insights."

He nodded somberly. "Sure, no problem."

The scent of dark roast coffee enveloped me as I stepped into the cozy warmth of the Seaview café. My eyes scanned the room, coming to rest on Leo.

He sat alone at a corner table, intently focused on his laptop screen, his brown hair tousled just so. I took a deep breath and headed his way, tightening my grip on the strap of my bag.

He glanced up as I approached, his piercing brown eyes moving across my face, assessing me like I was a puzzle he aimed to solve. I settled into the chair across from him without waiting for an invitation.

"You left this behind yesterday," I said, placing the leather notebook on the table. "Thought you'd want it back."

His gaze darted between me and the notebook, a flash of unease in his eyes. But it quickly vanished behind a mask of nonchalance. "I wasn't aware it was missing. Thank you..." He let the sentence hang there as if expecting me to finish it, an opening for me to divulge my name.

I obliged. "Audrey Fitzgerald, Private Investigator."

His eyes widened in surprise. I continued, "I know you were investigating Rayna Mills' affair with Blake Kingston. I thought he killed her, but his alibi is solid."

Leo nodded, intrigued. "Yes, I was compiling evidence for a story. Why come to me?"

I chose my words carefully. "I have... insider information that could break this open. But I need help to connect the dots."

His eyes glinted eagerly. "What kind of information?"

I hesitated. "I can't reveal my sources. But it gives me insights the police lack. If we combine my intel with your investigative skills, we have a real shot at solving this."

Leo leaned back, steepling his fingers as he assessed me. "So what's this 'insider information' you hint at but won't reveal?"

I met his gaze evenly. "Like I said, my sources must remain confidential for now. But I have details about Rayna's relationships and state of mind before her death that provide critical context."

He nodded slowly. "Things she shared with you directly?"

"In a manner of speaking," I said cryptically, maintaining my poker face. I couldn't risk exposing my gift, not to a reporter hungry for a scoop.

"And you really think combining your intel with my investigative skills will crack this case?" He eyed me doubtfully.

"I know you've been digging into Kingstons' motives and means," I pressed on. "But Rayna's perspective is missing. Together, we can get the full picture." I tapped the notebook meaningfully. "You're good, Leo. But even you hit dead ends trying to piece this together alone. With what I know, we have a real chance to find the truth."

He considered this, drumming his fingers on the table. Finally, he met my gaze, resolve sharpening his features.

"All right, Audrey, you've convinced me, as much as I dislike partnering with someone," he conceded. "I'm prepared to work with you to uncover Rayna's killer, but I get the scoop. Deal?"

I nodded. "Deal. Let's see what we can uncover together."

CHAPTER TEN

I queued up the CCTV footage Ben had sent to my laptop as Leo leaned in attentively. "My source sent this over. It's from the expo leading up to the fashion show."

The grainy video showed Blake's wife, Olivia, arguing heatedly with a blonde woman whose face wasn't visible. Their body language was tense and angry.

Leo studied it closely, eyes narrowed. "Hmm, any idea who blondie is there with Olivia?"

I shook my head. "Olivia claims it was just a random woman hassling her. But I'm not buying it."

"I agree. This seems personal." Leo tapped the screen. "You know, from the back, she looks a bit like Marianne Thompson, that designer. Could be her."

I considered this, intrigued. "Hmm. Maybe?"

Leo nodded, thoughtful. "Worth looking into both their connections."

"Definitely."

"So where do we go from here?" Leo asked, leaning back in his chair. "Who are our suspects? What are their motives?"

"Blake was my number one suspect, but his alibi checks out. Olivia says she has an alibi. The police are still checking. But I say she definitely has a motive."

Leo snorted. "Uh, you think? Finding out your husband is having an affair with a pretty young thing? People have killed for less."

"A crime of passion." I agreed. Then looked Leo dead in the eye. "And then there's you."

"Me?" He sat back, shocked. "You think I'm a suspect."

I was taking a chance, rolling the dice. This could go one of two ways. But he'd be smart enough to realize he was on the radar.

He chose wisely. "You think I raised the stakes on my exposé? Added murder to the affair story for fame and money?"

I shrugged. "I read your notes. You desperately

need money—gambling debts, Leo? Cliché for a reporter. Easy to imagine you spicing up your story with murder to make a name and clear debts."

"You're right. I could have. But I didn't." He met my gaze evenly. "Finding the truth matters more to me than a quick payout."

I nodded slowly. "Good. Then we still have an investigation to run."

My phone erupted to life, Seb's custom ringtone belting out, "It's Raining Men." I held up a finger to pause my conversation with Leo.

"Audrey, I come bearing good news and bad news." Seb's grave tone contrasted with the cheerful ringtone. "The good news is, your backyard is about to become a woodland fairy paradise…"

As he described the twinkling lights and flower garlands, I pictured my back garden transformed into a wedding nirvana. A benefit of getting married at home? Thor and Bandit got to share in our big day. I smiled, imagining tiny top hats perched between their ears.

"But—" Seb paused dramatically, and my shoulders tensed, waiting for the blow. "The caterers have come down with the plague. The wedding feast is no more."

My head fell into my hands. Of all the possible disasters...

"The CWA!" Leo blurted out. I lifted my head, puzzled. "Sorry. I couldn't help but overhear. Have them do a potluck. They can whip up a feast on the fly."

Brilliant. Seb agreed eagerly, then bid me adieu, no doubt to call the CWA chairwoman immediately. I slumped back, the rollercoaster of wedding planning draining me.

"When's the big day?" Leo asked.

"Tomorrow."

He nearly spit out his sip of coffee. "Tomorrow?"

I shook my head, already exhausted by his reaction. "Don't even."

Leo leaned forward, his eyes narrowing shrewdly. "Why are you here with me when you should be getting ready for your wedding? Cold feet?"

I crossed my arms. "Nope. My feet are toasty warm, thank you very much." I was not about to confess my real motivation—that solving Rayna's murder might mean one less ghost at my wedding.

"Seb has everything under control," I said, waving away Leo's insinuation. "But that reminds me, I wanted to ask you something."

Leo gestured for me to continue.

"What do you know about the Emily Carson case?"

His brows furrowed. "Name rings a bell."

"It's a cold case from Willow Creek. She was murdered after a photo shoot."

Leo rubbed his chin thoughtfully as I outlined the details. When I suggested the cases could be connected, his eyes lit up. Leo liked a challenge.

"With your investigative talents, maybe you could uncover any similarities beyond the obvious?" I proposed.

Leo nodded slowly, intrigued. "I'll take a look at the Emily Carson case. If there is a connection, it could be the missing link."

"Great," I said, closing my laptop and slipping it into my bag. "We should reconvene later to compare notes."

He nodded. "Deal. I'll text you the moment I find something interesting."

My phone buzzed on the table. I glanced at the screen: Kade.

"Hey, Babe. What's up?" I said, keeping my voice neutral. A knot of tension tightened in my stomach; I had a feeling this call signaled bad news.

"You're not going to believe this, Audrey," he said,

his voice tinged with urgency. "Olivia's alibi doesn't check out."

My heart skipped a beat. "What do you mean?"

"She claimed she was at a charity meeting, remember? Well, the organization says they haven't had a meeting in weeks. So, where was she?"

Chills raced down my spine. "So, she lied."

"It seems like it."

"What about Blake?"

"His alibi holds up, and his gun isn't a match. We're turning up the heat on Olivia now. I predict the Kingston's are going to lawyer up, in which case we won't be able to hold them here much longer."

I bit my lip, my mind racing. "Okay, thanks for letting me know. I'll dig a little deeper from my end."

As I hung up, Leo looked up from his laptop, sensing the gravity in my expression. "What happened?"

"Olivia's alibi just crumbled," I said, barely above a whisper, my fingers tapping on the tabletop.

Leo closed his laptop and leaned forward, the glint in his eyes unmistakable. "So, our charity queen isn't as benevolent as she pretends to be."

I nodded, my eyes meeting his. "Looks that way. It's more than enough to make her a prime suspect again."

Leo's eyes narrowed. "But the question remains, where was she if not at the charity meeting? And why lie about it?"

I pondered briefly, my intuition tingling with half-formed suspicions. "That's what we need to find out. But the police are on it. Right now, I have to trust that they'll do their job."

Leo raised an eyebrow. "So, what's next for you, then?"

"I've got a wedding to save," I said, exhaling deeply as I gathered my things. "Seb's been handling the chaos so far, but I need to go make sure everything's on track for tomorrow."

Leo looked up from his laptop; his expression turned serious. "All right, you handle your wedding, and I'll dig into Emily Carson's case. We'll meet up to compare notes?"

"Yep." I absently waved as I headed out the door, my mind racing with thoughts of a backyard wedding, potluck catering, and the reality that Olivia might not be as innocent as she claimed.

Sunlight streamed through the windows, warming the car interior as I navigated the streets. My fingers drummed on the steering wheel, tapping out a rhythm to a song only I could hear, but it did little to chase away the unease settling in my gut.

"You seem miles away," Ben's voice suddenly broke my reverie. I glanced to my right, unsurprised to find him occupying the passenger seat, dressed in his classic ensemble of a leather jacket and jeans.

"Yeah, well, today's been... complicated," I muttered, flipping on the turn signal as I approached an intersection.

Ben studied my face; concern etched in his features. "Leo's an unknown variable. You sure you want to involve him?"

"Is anyone ever really known?" I countered. "Besides, I need all the help I can get, and he has access to information I don't. We're on a time crunch here, Ben. You said you were going to check him out. What did you find?"

"I scoured his laptop. The piece he's writing about Blake Kingston is hot. He's taking his time with it. Methodical. He wants to back it up with solid proof."

"So he's not a hack?"

"I didn't say that. I found plenty of stories he's penned that have one foot firmly planted in fiction." He sighed, folding his arms across his chest. "Journalists, though—they're notorious for having their own agendas. And this guy's no exception."

The light turned green, and I pressed on the gas,

navigating through the crossroads. "I know, Ben, I know. But what choice do I have? If he's got information that can help solve Rayna's case, I can't just ignore that. Especially with the wedding breathing down my neck."

His eyes locked onto mine, serious and unwavering. "Fine. But if you're going to dance with the devil, make sure you're leading."

I chuckled at the imagery. "You taught me well, remember? I know how to keep my cards close."

Ben nodded, finally breaking into a half-smile. "Just making sure. You can never be too careful."

As I pulled into my driveway, the sunlight reflecting off the windows like tiny beacons, I felt a pang of gratitude for Ben's presence beside me. Whatever lay ahead, I wasn't facing it alone.

As soon as I unlocked the front door and stepped inside, a chorus of expectant meows and chittering greeted me. Thor, his gray fur slightly mussed as though he'd just woken from a nap, strolled up to me, trying to appear nonchalant but failing miserably. Bandit scampered beside him, her little raccoon eyes wide with excitement.

"Finally," Thor grumbled, his gaze intense. "I thought you'd never return. I'm starving."

"Hi, Mom! Hi! Hi!" Bandit chattered, hopping from one foot to the other.

I chuckled, bending down to pat them both. "I'm sure you two have been up to no good while I was gone."

Thor sniffed indignantly. "I am merely surviving, given that my daily rations have been reduced to nothing more than crumbs."

Bandit nodded, clearly taken in by Thor's dramatics. "He's really hungry, Mom. Really, really hungry!"

Rolling my eyes, I walked past them, heading for the kitchen. My wedding dress, hanging from the stairway railing, caught my eye, and I felt a flutter of excitement. Less than twenty-four hours, and I'd be wearing it for real.

Seb looked up from his planning station at the kitchen counter, papers strewn about in semi-organized chaos and grinned.

"Audrey! I have news!"

"Let me guess," I said, placing my bag on the counter. "You've somehow managed to get a national culinary award-winning chef to replace our plagued caterers?"

Seb's eyes twinkled. "Even better. The CWA ladies are all in for a potluck wedding feast! It's going to be fabulous, and it only cost us a 'modest' donation."

I laughed, relieved Leo's suggestion had paid off. "You're a miracle worker."

He waved it off. "Anything for your special day. And to keep Amanda from taking over with her peculiar ideas of what's 'suitable.'"

"That is indeed a cause worth fighting for," I said, meeting his eyes gratefully.

Seb suddenly looked more serious. "How goes the investigation? Any breakthroughs?"

I paused, hesitating. "It's complicated, but we're getting there."

Before he could press further, Thor sauntered in, Bandit trailing behind him. "In case you forgot, some of us are still waiting for sustenance."

I sighed. "Fine, you win. Let's get you something to eat before you wither away to nothing."

Thor nodded approvingly as if granting me a great honor. Bandit clapped her paws together, unable to contain her excitement.

"You see? This is why I adore weddings," Seb said, gesturing toward Thor and Bandit. "They're not just a union between two people, but a celebration of all the love that surrounds them."

I looked at Seb, then at Thor and Bandit, and felt

a swell of affection. He was right. Love surrounded me in its various, wonderful forms. And come what may, I wouldn't have it any other way.

CHAPTER ELEVEN

I was in the middle of choosing between two almost identical shades of pink nail polish for the wedding when my phone buzzed. The screen displayed Leo's name. I sighed and picked up.

"Leo, my wedding is tomorrow. Please tell me you're calling with good news," I said as I picked up the call.

"I found a connection. How about a sit-down with Marianne Thompson at Éclat Designs? Today at four."

"The Marianne Thompson, who designed the dresses for both our victims?" I asked.

"The very same."

"I'm there."

Walking into Éclat Designs felt like stepping into a living Pinterest board. Elegant and edgy, each dress stood like a museum piece. The scent of lilac floated in the air.

Marianne Thompson greeted us, her platinum pixie cut perfect, her oversized glasses making a fashion statement all their own. "Ah, Audrey and Leo, it's a pleasure to meet you in person. You don't seem as intimidating as I thought you would be."

Her compliment, if you could call it that, hung awkwardly in the air. Leo and I exchanged a glance.

"Let's get down to business, shall we?" Leo navigated us to the plush chairs and the very fragile-looking glass table between them.

Marianne's tone switched as soon as we sat. She explained her designs with a fervor that bordered on religious. But when Leo probed about her connection to Lumina Models, she faltered. "Well, business is business. You find your allies where you can."

"And have any of your 'allies' turned into enemies lately? Anyone not thrilled about your participation in the expo?" I asked.

Her eyes darted to a stack of papers on her desk,

then back to us. "I've received some anonymous messages asking me to pull out. The police are treating them as idle threats."

The way she casually dismissed the threats but visibly checked her papers spoke volumes. She was hiding something—or at least highly selective about what she let on.

I crossed my legs, feeling the tension ratchet up a notch. "Marianne, you have a successful boutique, your designs have a strong following, and yet, you're receiving threats. Are we to believe that these are just the usual business grudges?"

She sighed, took off her glasses, and cleaned them with a cloth, avoiding eye contact. "In this industry, everyone has enemies. Competition is fierce. But I've built Éclat Designs from the ground up, and I won't let a few ominous words derail that."

I glanced at Leo; he was scribbling notes. "Do you mind if we take a look at those messages?"

Marianne replaced her glasses and hesitated for a split second as if weighing her options. Then she retrieved the papers. As she handed them to me, I noticed a tremor in her hand, a flash of something unsettled in her eyes before her composed mask fell back into place. "Here. Take them. But they won't lead you to anything I haven't already told the police."

I quickly skimmed through the papers. The threats were vague but menacing, telling Marianne to pull out of the expo or face "irreparable damage."

"Marianne, these threats mention 'irreparable damage.' That seems quite severe," Leo pointed out.

"Yes, but who hasn't had their work criticized?" She chuckled nervously, but the tension was palpable. "Maybe it's another designer who's afraid of a little competition or a jilted ex-model. Who knows?"

I studied her. Her casual demeanor couldn't completely hide a certain edge in her voice, an undercurrent of defensiveness. My eyes landed on an intricately beaded dress displayed in the corner, its precise beading leaving no thread out of place.

"That's a show-stopping design," I commented.

Marianne followed my gaze. "Thank you."

"Have you ever considered that these threats could be serious? Given the tragic events surrounding your recent designs," Leo pressed.

She sighed, finally breaking her well-practiced composure. "Yes, okay? But what am I to do? Drop everything, shut down the shop? That would be giving in to fear. And I've fought too hard to let fear dictate my actions now."

"Fair point," Leo said as he took the printout of threats from me, flipping through the pages. "But it might be wise to take these threats a bit more seriously, given the circumstances."

Marianne nodded as if she'd just been reminded of the weight of the situation. "I'll consider it."

I glanced around the boutique again, scrutinizing every detail. I spied an overflowing wastebasket; fabric swatches peeking out. Curious, I leaned over for a better look, spotting threads and beads amongst the scraps spilling over the edge and scattered on the floor. Odd for a designer so meticulous in her work to display signs of disorganization.

As Leo and I exited the shop, my mind was filled with doubts. Marianne seemed to have a hidden agenda; her suave demeanor and outward friendliness masked something more complicated underneath. She wanted us to believe only what she chose to show, nothing beyond that.

Once we were safely away from Éclat Designs, Leo turned to me, his brows knitted in a frown of skepticism. "What's your take on Marianne? Could these threats somehow tie back to Olivia?"

I shrugged, still processing the odd dynamic of our meeting with the designer. "Honestly? Olivia threatening Marianne doesn't quite add up. Olivia has her faults—oh, believe me, she has faults—but orchestrating threats over a fashion show doesn't seem her style. Plus, Olivia has her own troubles now with the police breathing down her neck."

Leo nodded, flipping through his notepad as if it could magically supply a missing link. "Yeah, agreed. We don't have a direct connection, and the motive is shaky at best. Olivia gains nothing from Marianne pulling out of the expo."

I leaned against the car, mulling over our list of suspects. "Could someone else have a vested interest in scaring Marianne?"

"I've been pondering that. But if Olivia isn't behind it, then who? A random designer she's edged out in the past?" Leo shrugged, clearly frustrated.

It was like fitting pieces into a jigsaw puzzle, except some of the pieces had been deliberately mis-cut. "You know, there's something unsettling about Marianne. She seemed... careful. Guarded. Like she was more concerned with how much we could discover rather than finding the person making these threats."

Leo looked up from his notepad, his eyes narrowing. "You think she's hiding something?"

"I can't put my finger on it," I admitted. "But I don't think we've seen all the cards she's holding."

He nodded. "Okay, say Marianne is the crafty one here. How do we prove it?"

"We need to verify the threats. They were emails, so tracing their origin could give us more clues. Maybe we can find who sent them."

"Ah, the classic 'unmask the villain by tracking down the IP address' move. I like it," Leo grinned.

Little did Leo know I had a ghostly sidekick who excelled at that very thing. As soon as Ben put in another appearance, I'd have him chase down Marianne's emails.

My reflection in the mirror was a disaster—hair sticking up in odd places, no makeup, and I was still in my robe. "Come on, Audrey, get it together," I muttered to myself. I had fifteen minutes to look like a person who had her life sorted out—or at least one who could dress herself.

After a frantic search, I finally picked out a simple blue dress. It was nothing compared to

Amanda's ensembles, but it would have to do. I stepped into the dress, zipped it up, and dabbed some makeup on my face. One last glance at the mirror confirmed I looked, well, presentable enough for family.

My phone buzzed on the bathroom counter. The message was from an unknown number. *Meet me at the abandoned warehouse on Birch Street at midnight. I have information on Rayna's murder. Tell no one, especially the cops.* I felt the chill of those words crawl up my spine. Who could this be? But there was no time to ponder; I was already late.

Arriving at my parents' house, I braced myself for the familial circus. Amanda was the first to greet me, radiating an air of pristine motherhood with Laura's youngest, baby Grace, cooing on her hip.

"Audrey! You're late and disheveled," she pointed out, eyeing me critically.

"Thanks, Amanda. You look... flawless as usual," I deflected with a tight smile.

Inside, the air was thick with the smell of roast beef and the cacophony of family banter. I made my rounds, knocking over a vase filled with fresh daisies in the process. "Oh, Audrey," Mom sighed, dabbing at the puddle with a kitchen towel as if performing a sacred ritual.

I caught Amanda side-eyeing me, no doubt making another tally mark on her mental list of how she was going to cure me of my clumsiness once and for all.

As I moved toward the dining room, I saw Seb laughing between my dad and Dennis, Kade's dad. They were in a heated discussion about organic gardening, of all things. Sylvia, Kade's mom, winked at me approvingly.

Dustin was busy with Madeline and Nathaniel, his hands moving in a choreographed ballet of parenting: cutting chicken here, wiping a mouth there. As I passed by, he handed me Isabelle, Laura's eldest, who promptly used my hair as a pasta-tossing catapult.

I caught Dustin's eye and sent him a telepathic SOS, but he was deep in the Zen art of toddler wrangling. Isabelle's little fingers were pasta-painters, and my hair was the canvas. Oh, the sacrifices of aunthood!

Finally, after a noodle hit a wall and slid down dramatically—think slow-mo action scene—I knew something had to give. I looked down at Isabelle and smiled, deciding to go for the hand-off, the old pass-the-potato move. At the perfect moment, when Dustin's hands were miraculously free for 2.5

seconds, I slid Isabelle back into the nook of his arm.

"Here ya go, hot potato," I quipped. As I retreated, I plucked a noodle from my hair, wondering just how much Isabelle had managed to stash in there before I'd managed to hand her off.

While I was foraging for rogue spaghetti, the door swung open, and Kade walked in. His eyes met mine, and he crossed the room as if propelled by an invisible force. He wrapped me in his arms and kissed me like he hadn't seen me in weeks—deep, long, and full of promise. The room disappeared, and it was just the two of us.

"God, I needed that," he murmured, breaking away just enough to speak.

"I've missed you too," I said, feeling a brief respite from the emotional turmoil of the day.

He looked me over, his brow furrowed in concern. "You look... tired. Stressed."

I hesitated for a split second, the anonymous text message flashing in my mind. "Ah, you know, lack of sleep. Ben threw a fashion parade in the middle of the night," I half-joked, "and this case isn't exactly a walk in the park."

As Kade and I stood wrapped in our bubble of affection, I noticed our families' reactions out of the corner of my eye. My mother had a tissue dabbed to her eyes, always sentimental when it came to her kids. Dad grinned like he'd won a jackpot, proudly nodding at Kade as if to say, 'Good job, son.'

Across the room, Kade's parents, Dennis and Sylvia, exchanged a meaningful look. Sylvia's eyes twinkled, mirroring the diamond earrings she wore. Dennis offered a subdued but approving nod, the corners of his mouth lifting in a smile. The kind that said, 'This is what we flew across the country to see.'

Laura caught my eye and mouthed, 'So cute.' Meanwhile, Brad was too engrossed in stopping Isabelle from throwing mashed potatoes to notice.

Amanda, immaculate as ever, held Nathaniel on her lap and looked on with a restrained smile, probably making mental notes on how she could make the scene even more perfect—like adding rose petals or harmonizing violins in the background.

Dustin, who'd always been protective of me, watched Kade for a long moment before giving him a hard slap on the back that said, 'You better take care of my sister,' as much as it said, 'welcome to the family.'

Breaking away from our private moment, Kade and I rejoined our families, slipping back into the dinner chaos like we'd never left. But that brief interlude had recharged me, and as we sat down to eat, I felt a renewed sense of hope and belonging— like whatever challenges lay ahead, we would face them together.

We settled into dessert—homemade apple pie and vanilla ice cream. I was handed the serving spoon and, in a move that surprised no one, dropped a dollop of ice cream right into my lap.

"Here, Audrey," Amanda chirped, extending a wet wipe as if offering a lifeline. "You should really keep these in your purse."

"Brilliant," I said, scrubbing at the cold, melting blob.

Dinner gave way to after-dinner coffee, the adults segregating into little gossip clusters in the living room. Isabelle and Grace were put to bed, Madeline was coloring, and Nathaniel had found fascination with a spoon.

My phone buzzed again. The same unknown number. *Remember, midnight. Birch Street.*

"Who was that?" Kade asked, noticing my distraction with my phone.

"No one," I lied, tucking the phone back into my purse and sliding my hand into his. Kade lifted our clasped hands and dropped a kiss on the back of my hand before turning to respond to his dad, who was asking something about a tour of the police station.

Glancing around the room, I felt an intense love for this sprawling, imperfect family. Sylvia was discussing wedding florals with Mom, Seb was immersed in a conversation with Laura about the Sex in the City remake, and Amanda—well, Amanda was organizing Mom's cutlery drawer.

CHAPTER TWELVE

*L*eaving a scribbled note on the kitchen counter—*Gone for a quick drive back soon*—I grabbed my keys and purse and slipped out of the house. My phone showed 11:45 p.m. I had fifteen minutes to get to Birch Street, a part of town you wouldn't want to visit without a full can of pepper spray and a Kevlar vest.

The drive was tense, my fingers drumming on the steering wheel to the rhythm of the pounding in my chest. It was 11:55 p.m. on the nose when I pulled up, cutting the engine. Streetlights were conspicuously absent, as if even they didn't dare hang around here after dark.

Exiting the car, I locked it behind me.

The air hung still as if it was afraid to disturb the

silent atmosphere. Buildings slouched in disrepair, windows boarded up or shattered, graffiti scrawling out unreadable tags. A stray dog howled in the distance, creating a stereotypical—but not comforting—soundtrack.

I took a deep breath, regretting it instantly as the scent of trash and decay filled my nostrils. "Even the airs past its sell-by date," I said to myself, my voice shaking more than I'd like to admit.

Pulling up the flashlight app, I held my phone aloft like the torch of Lady Liberty—if Lady Liberty was dressed in a wrinkled t-shirt and old jeans.

The silence of the night was deafening, every rustle in the bushes growing tenaciously amongst the abandoned buildings, echoing like a scream in my ears. I dug around in my purse, pushing aside a tube of mascara and a half-eaten granola bar until I found my bright pink Taser.

I gripped the taser tightly, its absurd color somehow reassuring. "I'm ready, you anonymous coward. Show yourself," I hissed.

Minutes stretched longer than a Monday morning. Nothing moved, and the suspense was gnawing at me. I took a few cautious steps forward. That's when I heard it—a soft whispering sound, like footsteps crunching on gravel.

My heart rate went from "aerobic workout" to "rocket launch." Holding my breath, I turned slowly, my flashlight slicing through the darkness.

Nothing. No one.

"Okay, Audrey. Get a grip. You solve murders; you can handle this," I muttered, tucking a wild strand of hair behind my ear. But as my hand returned to the taser, a swift movement caught my eye—a flicker of shadow that didn't belong.

Something was definitely there.

I raised my taser, finger hovering over the trigger, my every instinct screaming at me to run. But then a twig snapped behind me. Whipping around, I tripped over my own feet and stumbled, sending my taser flying out of my hand.

As it hit the ground, it activated, sending a buzzing arc of electricity into a bush. The bush didn't seem to appreciate it, its leaves rustling as if in indignation.

"Fantastic. I just tased a plant," I sighed, picking up my dignity and then the taser. But as I stood, the whispering sound returned—louder now, undeniably the sound of footsteps.

This was it. Heart in my throat, I whirled around, taser making contact. A yelp pierced the night air, followed by a thud.

Cautiously, I shined the phone's flashlight on the person I'd just electrocuted. "Kade?!"

He was sprawled on the ground, twitching slightly. "Audrey, what the—? I thought we were at the 'for better or worse' stage, not the 'til death do us part.'"

I crouched down, stammering. "Oh my God, I'm so sorry! What are you doing here?"

"Following my future wife, who's sneaking out of the house at midnight," he said, struggling to sit up. "You've been acting strange all evening. Then you rush off into the night, to the sketchiest part of town, no less. What's going on, Audrey?"

I hesitated, biting my lower lip. "I received an anonymous tip about the murder. They told me to come here alone."

He looked at me, his eyes softening. "Audrey, we're getting married. That means facing danger together, not running off into dark alleys alone. Especially with your aim."

"Fair call."

Then my phone buzzed. It was another anonymous text: "*You're not alone. Meeting canceled.*"

I showed Kade the message. His eyes narrowed. "We can't ignore this, Audrey. Whoever this is, they're messing with a police investigation and your safety."

I felt a chill crawl up my spine. "What are we going to do?"

"I'll brief the guys at the station in the morning. I still need to hand over a couple of things despite being on leave, but this needs to stay between us. I don't want you to be more exposed than necessary."

I pressed my lips together, contemplating. "Do you think we'll get this resolved in time?" I'd been hoping my rendezvous with the tipster would have led to a breakthrough in the case and Rayna's murder would be solved, wrapped up in a pretty bridal bow. It was looking more and more likely that wasn't going to happen—Kade and I were set to walk down the aisle at sunset tomorrow, less than twenty-four hours from now.

Kade looked deep into my eyes, his expression unreadable for a heartbeat before settling on reassurance. "We will, Audrey. We'll solve this case, and nothing's going to stop us from walking down that aisle together."

"Let's get you back to your car," he added, walking toward where he'd parked discreetly enough that I hadn't noticed until now.

We walked in silence, the air still thick with the

night's events. I couldn't shake off the feeling that someone had been watching us. Our mysterious texter had canceled the meeting because Kade was with me. That thought alone was enough to give me goosebumps.

As we reached my car, Kade seemed to sense my lingering disquiet. "You okay?"

I forced a smile. "Just another day in Cozyville, huh?"

He chuckled. "Yeah, where tasering your fiancé is considered foreplay."

I got into my car, putting the key into the ignition but pausing before turning it. "Thanks for coming after me tonight, Kade."

Kade's eyebrows drew together as he looked through my car window, his eyes softening from cop to fiancé in a heartbeat. "That's not going to be a habit, okay? From here on out, we face things together."

"Together," I echoed, the word wrapping around us like a vow.

A shiver that seemed to radiate from the depths of Antarctica crept up my foot. "Ben, for the love of—"

I jerked my leg, pulling my knee toward my chest. The sudden jolt sent me tumbling out of bed in a graceless heap. Thor opened one orange eye and looked at me with disgust before settling back into the tangle of sheets. Bandit blinked in bemusement from her perch on my pillow.

"Ah, you're up! Bright-eyed and bushy-tailed!" Ben materialized beside the bed.

I glared at him as I picked myself off the floor. "Where have you been? I had work for you."

"Ah, just catching the last few episodes of 'Love Island' over at Mrs. Thompson's place. You should see her home cinema set-up!"

"Fantastic," I mumbled, pulling a robe around me as I headed downstairs to the kitchen. I opened the fridge, its shelves overflowing with wedding prep food. Shuffling items around, I moved a jug of orange juice to grab the milk and absentmindedly held it out to Ben. "Hold this a sec."

The jug plummeted to the floor, shattering and splattering orange juice everywhere. Fantastic.

Seconds later, Kade came thundering down the stairs. "Audrey! Are you okay?"

I sighed, stepping around the shards of glass floating in the orange lake that now covered the floor. "I'm fine. My pride, however, has suffered irreparable damage."

Kade led me to the sofa, sitting me down before heading back to clean the mess. "Stay put. I've got this."

As he started mopping, I turned to Ben. "Could you do me a favor and check Marianne Thompson's emails? Someone's been sending her threats, telling her to pull out of the expo. I want to know who."

"Can do," Ben said, saluting before fading away.

Kade returned with a cup of coffee, handing it to me with a gentle smile. "You're running on fumes, Audrey."

I sipped the coffee, relishing its warmth but mostly it's caffeine. He wasn't wrong. I felt like a zombie that had been binge-watching a Netflix series all night—except, you know, without the craving for brains. My eyelids were staging a mutiny, refusing to stay open, and I was pretty sure my yawns were threatening to dislocate my jaw. If sleep were a currency, I'd be filing for bankruptcy. Heck, even my coffee was looking at me like, "Girl, I can only do so much."

"Why are you even up?" Kade asked, sitting next to me and pulling me to his side.

"Ben woke me up. He's been MIA, and I needed

him to do some of his electronic data magic." I wiggled my fingers in the air to demonstrate. "I don't know how he knows when I need him, but he knows. I guess he didn't pick up on the sense of urgency this time, though."

Kade snorted. "What was he watching this time?"

"Love Island."

Exhausted but still buzzing, Kade and I slouched deeper into the sofa. "Honestly, Audrey, how can you not see the appeal of Love Island? It's like a human behavioral study with cocktails," Kade defended, his eyes half-lidded.

"Ah yes, a high-brow educational experience, sandwiched between swimsuits and drama," I retorted, sarcasm dripping from every word. Within minutes, we'd both succumbed to the comforting embrace of sleep, curled up together like two exhausted peas in a pod.

A loud knock rattled the back door, jolting us awake and sending Thor and Bandit into a state of alarmed fluffiness. Kade checked his watch. "Seb's early. He said he wouldn't be here until eight."

Rubbing my eyes, I got up to answer the door. Seb burst in, arms full of flower arrangements and a clipboard dangling from one finger. "Audrey, darling, today's the day! Now, out, out, out! I can't have you lifting a finger or seeing the garden before it's perfect."

Kade stood up, stretching. "Seb's right, Audrey. Take the day to relax. I have to swing by the station anyway to check on a few things."

Seb handed me a set of keys. "My sanctuary is yours for the day. I've stocked the fridge, and there's a selection of herbal teas and bath bombs. Indulge."

I hesitated. The last time I'd been in that house, Ethel Hill tried to turn me into a permanent resident —in the most deadly way. "Well, if it's all the same to you, I might just stay—"

Seb cut me off. "Absolutely not! Today is about you, not to-do lists or murderers. My home is your Zen zone today. No arguments."

Kade kissed my forehead. "Seb's right. You deserve a break. As much as I'd love to join you, I'm catching up with my folks after I check in at work."

Sighing, I realized they had a point. "Okay, okay, I surrender. To next door I go, to a house filled with blissful memories of attempted murder."

Seb gave me a cheeky grin. "Oh, don't be so dramatic. After today, it'll be filled with memories of your perfect wedding eve."

After hurriedly changing into a t-shirt and shorts, I took the keys, kissed Kade goodbye, and reluctantly headed to Seb's. Sometimes surrendering is the bravest thing you can do— especially when faced with floral arrangements and Sebastian Castle.

Stepping into Seb's house felt like entering an entirely new realm—part nostalgia, part fabulous transformation. Ethel Hill's lavender and beeswax aroma had been replaced by a fresh blend of citrus and vanilla. Gone were the doilies and vases; in their stead were stylish glass sculptures and abstract art that screamed 'Seb.'

While Ethel's cottage core essence still lingered in the bones of the house, Seb had brought his own brand of fabulousness to it. The floral and lace theme was ousted in favor of bold prints and colors. Velvet cushions and plush throws graced the sofa, replacing the previous overtly feminine vibe with a touch of flamboyant sophistication.

The dining room, once dominated by an oval table dressed in lace, now featured a sleek glass table surrounded by contemporary chairs. The cumbersome lace curtains were replaced with sheer, flowing drapes that allowed plenty of light in, showcasing the still-charming country-style garden that he'd tastefully updated with pops of color and some exotic plants.

The galley kitchen had also received a Seb makeover. The end doors remained, but the countertops that once housed miniature pugs now featured chic canisters and a Nespresso machine. And bless Seb for that; if there was ever a day I needed a high-quality caffeine injection, it was today.

CHAPTER THIRTEEN

*S*teaming espresso in hand, I savored that fleeting moment of calm. Ah, caffeine. You beautiful, dark elixir. My phone buzzed abruptly on the marble kitchen counter, shattering the peace. Laura's name lit up the screen.

"Good morning! Where are you getting ready for the big day?" she chirped from the other end.

"At my place because the dress is there, and it's just easier," I told her, taking another sip of the rich coffee. "You're still coming over early to help me get ready, aren't you?" Navigating a wedding gown solo seemed like a one-way ticket to a clumsy disaster.

"I'm your maid of honor. Of course, I am."

Exhaling, I felt a weight lift. "Good. See you in a few hours."

"Can't wait, sis!" Laura said before we hung up. Her enthusiasm was infectious, even if my mind was juggling a thousand other pieces—some more grim than others.

The familiar ring of Donna Summer's "Last Dance" chimed through the air as Seb's doorbell went off. Grinning, I set my cup down on the counter. You couldn't just walk into Seb's house; you had to make a grand entrance whether or not you intended to.

Figuring it was a delivery for the wedding, I hurried to unlock the door, but when I swung it open, my eyes met with Olivia Kingston's. Her normally poised face looked flushed, her eyes red and teary. The abrupt shift from expecting a wedding delivery to facing a potential murder suspect had me on edge instantly.

"What do you want, Olivia?" I asked, keeping my voice level.

"We need to talk," she nearly spat, storming past me into Seb's living room as if she owned the place.

"Okay, let's talk." I followed her, my own emotional gears shifting from fatigue to high alert.

"You've ruined my life, Audrey. Ruined it! Ever since you started looking into Rayna's death, my life has been picked apart by the police, the media, and the damn town gossip. Is that what you wanted?"

My jaw clenched. "I'm not here to ruin anyone's life. I'm here to find out who took Rayna's."

"While dragging my name through the mud?" Olivia glared at me. "I've lost friends over this. People look at me differently. My marriage—" her voice broke.

I caught movement from the corner of my eye and turned to see Rayna and Emily walk through the wall to join us. They positioned themselves like spectators at a tennis match, clearly relishing the unfolding drama. Emily mimed munching on popcorn, her eyes twinkling.

"Do go on; this is getting juicy," Rayna said, waving her hand to encourage me to continue the conversation with Olivia.

"Are you even listening to me?" Olivia snapped, pulling my attention back to her.

"I am. But you need to understand if you didn't kill Rayna, you have nothing to worry about."

"That's easy for you to say!" Olivia's eyes narrowed. "I knew about Blake's affair, okay? I had my own investigator following him long before Rayna was killed."

That was a detail I hadn't expected. "Why didn't you come forward with this information sooner?"

"Would you?" she shot back. "Admitting that to the police would be like painting a bullseye on my own back."

Emily giggled at that, causing Rayna to shoot her a mock, scornful look.

"I don't know if I should believe you, Olivia. But that's not even for me to decide. If you've got a legitimate alibi, let's hear it."

Olivia sighed deeply, almost deflating in front of me. "I just want my life back, Audrey. If you're really hell-bent on solving this murder, then go solve it, but leave me out of it."

She walked out of Seb's house, leaving me standing there, torn between the urgency of solving the murder and the remnants of normalcy that I was trying to cling to just hours before my wedding.

I closed the door behind her, her perfume still hanging heavy in the air. Leaning against the door, I exhaled a sigh that carried both relief and concern.

"Wow, talk about drama," Ben said, materializing beside me.

"More like an emotional landmine," I replied, finally peeling myself away from the door.

"That was an A-grade freakout," Emily said, still

pretending to munch on her imaginary popcorn. Rayna gave Emily a sidelong glance. "No one does emotional wreckage like you, Emily."

"Though I must say, she has glorious hair," Emily said a tad wistfully.

"And what's that got to do with anything?" I asked, almost laughing. Although Emily wasn't wrong. Olivia Kingston was always immaculately presented, and despite her emotion and agitation, today was no different.

"In our line of work? Everything," Rayna winked. "But seriously, Audrey, you should get to the bottom of this before you say 'I do.'"

My head hung low, and a wave of weary fatigue came over me. I raised my hand to the back of my neck, massaging the tight muscles there with a sigh. "Thanks for that red-hot tip."

"This changes things. If Olivia was spying on Blake, she had the opportunity to plan something," Ben said.

"Or she's telling the truth," I mused, "and we've been chasing the wrong suspect." Picking up my now lukewarm cup of coffee, I took a sip before placing it back on the counter. "I've got a wedding to prepare for, a murder to solve, and less than ten hours for both. Fan-freakin'-tastic."

Seb came tearing through the back door, a whirlwind of energy, clipboard in hand. "Just checking in, you all okay here?" He didn't give me the opportunity to answer, his eyes scanning the list on his clipboard. "Wooden chairs and tables are arriving now for your back garden oasis," he checked off. "The arch is here; just need to zhoosh it up; boxes and boxes of decorations have arrived—I must say it was very fortuitous that the expo closed early, Audrey; I snagged some magnificent bargains from vendors wanting to offload stock rather than haul it all back home." He glanced up, gave a decisive nod, then breezed out, leaving me with my mouth hanging open.

Rayna and Emily cheered. Emily even threw her imaginary popcorn into the air.

"See? Good things are happening," Ben tried to reassure me.

I managed a smile. "Well, if the universe is trying to balance out, it better work overtime. Because right now, my life's like a seesaw and not the fun kind."

Ben moved closer, his eyes softening. "Hey, no matter what happens, you're getting married. And we'll solve this case, I promise."

I looked into his eyes and smiled. "I know we will." We always did.

"All right, team, let's get this bride ready for her big day—and catch a killer." I dialed Kade's number, tucking a loose strand of hair behind my ear as I waited for him to pick up. On the third ring, his voice filled the air.

"Hey, love. Everything okay?"

His voice was like comfort food, a balm to the day's anxieties.

"I miss you," I sighed. "I know we're not meant to see each other today, but I'd much rather spend the day with you."

He chuckled. "They say it's bad luck to see the bride before the wedding, but I could never consider myself unlucky when I'm with you."

I smiled, my heart swelling. "Listen, I need a favor. Could you grab my laptop from the home office? Seb's got the place looking like a floral battleground, and I can't get near it."

"Sure, I'll swing by and get it. You're at Seb's, right?"

"Yeah. Can't wait to see you, even if it's just a quick handoff."

He paused, and for a moment, the line went silent except for our soft breathing. "Me too, Audrey. Me too. See you soon."

The call ended, and I stared at the screen for a

second before pocketing the phone. Ben grinned from across the room, setting aside the ghostly bridal magazine he'd been flicking through.

"Guess he's as smitten with you as you are with him," he quipped.

I rolled my eyes but couldn't suppress my smile. "Hilarious. Now, let's get ready to dig into some data. We've got a murder to solve and not a lot of time to do it."

Twenty minutes later, Donna Summer's "Last Dance" reverberated through the room once more. Jumping to my feet, I hurried to the door, swinging it open. And there was Kade. His face broke into a grin at the sight of me. Our eyes met, and for a second, the world around us blurred. Then, like magnets, we were pulled toward each other. Our lips met in a kiss that was as quick as it was passionate. We pulled apart, our breaths quickening, faces flushed. "No bad luck today," I whispered, looking up into his eyes.

Kade's fingers brushed mine as he handed over the laptop bag. Electricity surged through me, a small but potent reminder of what awaited us at the end of this whirlwind day.

"I couldn't help myself," he whispered, his breath warm against my cheek. "I had to steal a kiss."

"No stealing required; I'll hand 'em over for free to you any day," I replied, my voice barely a whisper.

Emily made a heart shape with her hands, mouthing the word "Aww." Rayna sniffed and turned away.

"Sorry to break up the love fest," Ben interjected, "but tick-tock lovebirds. Murder's not going to solve itself."

Kade stepped back. "I've got to head back. My parents are in town. You know how it is."

"I do," I nodded, unzipping the laptop bag and pulling out my computer. "Go spend some time with them. We've got this end covered."

As Kade walked away, he turned back for a last look. "I'll see you at the altar."

"Cannot wait," I answered, my smile so wide my cheeks hurt.

The moment the door closed behind Kade, the room's energy shifted like the air itself was holding its breath.

Fingers dancing across the keyboard, I pulled up the digital mound of evidence related to Olivia. Photos, emails, phone records—all spread across the screen like an open dossier.

"Find anything interesting?" Ben walked over

and stood behind the couch, peering over my shoulder.

"Working on it," I murmured, my eyes darting across the screen. "After Olivia's unsettling visit this morning, my gut tells me something's off."

Ben pointed at the cell tower pings on the screen. "Speaking of Olivia, you might want to look at this. According to these records, she wasn't where she claimed to be. She said she left the expo before the fashion show, yet her phone puts her still at the expo."

I leaned in, eyes narrowing. "You're right. Maybe she left her phone behind?"

Ben shot me a look that said he thought my theory stinks. "Really, Fitz? That's what you're going with? She left her phone behind?"

"Not intentionally," I protested. "You can't deny the CCTV footage shows her leaving the expo well before the fashion parade. But if her phone is still pinging off the closest tower, then yeah, maybe she dropped it, misplaced it, something."

"Surely she'd have mentioned that when questioned?"

I shrugged. "Maybe she did. I don't know what she's told the police—and don't ask me to ask Kade. He's officially off duty."

"He may not be at work, but I bet he's still working just like you are. Come on, Fitz, he's a detective; his dad is a retired cop. It's in their blood. I bet they're doing exactly what you are, trying to solve this puzzle before we run out of day."

"What I don't get is why Olivia turned up here, accusing me of ruining her life, if she's the guilty party. If she killed Rayna, why would she even turn up here? Surely she'd keep her distance?"

Rayna and Emily claimed spots on the couch as if it were a front-row seat to a Broadway show. Rayna twirled a lock of her hair. "A woman with a secret is a dangerous thing."

Emily chuckled beside her. "The drama just keeps on coming, doesn't it?"

"Why would Olivia lie?" The question hung in the air, tinged with the tension of her recent visit. "If she can't be truthful about her whereabouts, what else is she hiding?"

"Could she be covering for someone?" Ben suggested.

Emily grinned. "Oh, I love a good plot twist."

I sat silently, remembering what Olivia had said earlier. That my investigation was ruining her life. A shiver of responsibility trickled down my spine.

"You okay there?" Ben asked, noticing the cloud that seemed to hang over me.

"Am I doing the right thing?" I murmured, staring at the screen, which displayed emails, phone records, and hastily written notes that felt like an intrusion into people's private lives. "What if I'm just stirring the pot for everyone, especially Olivia?"

Rayna crossed her arms. "You're chasing justice, Audrey. That's always worth the effort."

Emily was back to miming eating popcorn. "Doing the right thing isn't always the easiest thing. But it's still the right thing."

My fingers hovered over the touchpad, ready to close the evidence files. But something caught my eye—a string of text messages between Olivia and an unknown number.

"Hey, what's this?" I clicked on the thread, reading through cryptic exchanges that hinted at a clandestine meeting. "These messages were sent on the day of the murder."

Rayna leaned over to read. "Who's the unknown number?"

"Don't know, but I can find out," Ben offered, enthusiasm lighting up his face. "The point is, you're onto something. You're not just stirring the pot;

you're pulling back layers that people have tried hard to keep hidden."

"I need to talk to her and Blake again," I said, my decision final as I shut my laptop. "I can't let this go, especially not today."

Ben echoed what I was thinking. "The wedding is in a few hours, Audrey. Time's ticking."

Emily chimed in, "I can't wait to see you solve this in your wedding dress."

Rayna looked amused. "Quite the spectacle that would be."

"It's risky," I admitted, "but if Olivia's the killer, I have to find out, wedding or no wedding."

"Refill, anyone?" Emily joked, pretending to toss imaginary popcorn into her mouth.

CHAPTER FOURTEEN

I slid my laptop closed, my fingers drumming nervously on the lid as I mentally calculated how much time I had up my sleeve.

Rayna chose that moment to lean back with an overly dramatic sigh and declare, "Oh, honey, if you think the fashion industry is all glitz and glamor, you're sorely mistaken."

"What?" I had no clue what she was talking about. My mind was busy juggling my imminent wedding and busting Olivia for Rayna's murder when she piped up with useless trivia about the fashion industry.

Rayna laughed, a silvery sound that clashed with the mood. "Oh, you know. Backstabbings, silent treatments, the occasional—" She paused as if searching for the right word. "—disappearances."

That caught my attention. "Disappearances?"

Rayna tossed her hair. "Not literal ones. It's more like being vanished from the scene. Careers crushed, reputations ruined, that sort of thing. Even queens can fall, you know."

Emily tossed more popcorn into her mouth. "Like Olivia, you mean?"

"Wait. What?" My eyes went from Rayna to Emily and back again. Surely they weren't saying...

Rayna stood and began pacing, her expression turning into a smirk. "Ever wondered why I was Blake's side piece? It's because he loves models. His wife was one. But she aged out. I was the new, improved version."

My eyes widened in surprise before quickly narrowing with suspicion. I inhaled sharply, my temper rising as I asked, "Olivia used to be a model? Why didn't you mention this earlier?" My brows drew together, and my mouth formed a thin line of disbelief as I stared at them both.

Rayna shrugged, a glimmer of delight in her eyes. "I only just thought of it. Blake pursued me because I reminded him of Olivia when she was fresh on the runway."

"So, you weren't trying to one-up Olivia by snagging her husband?"

Rayna chuckled, her laughter as icy as her demeanor. "Oh, honey, if I wanted to one-up Olivia, I wouldn't need her husband to do it. Blake came after me because he missed the youthful version of his wife. But you know, the industry has a way of replacing yesterday's faces."

"Anything else you've forgotten to tell me?" I grumbled, silently seething that Rayna was so self-absorbed she was only just now thinking of sharing pertinent information. Information that could lead to catching her killer.

Shooting me a frosty glare, she disappeared.

The room fell into silence until a quiet sigh escaped Emily's lips. As I glanced up at her, I saw the softness in her eyes. "You know Rayna," she said. "She can be incredibly self-centered, but deep down, she's trying to protect something. She just has a twisted way of showing it."

The tightness in my chest grew with each passing second as exasperation and anger bubbled inside me. My hands curled into fists at the thought of someone holding back information that could help solve their own murder. I let out a frustrated sigh, feeling like I was running out of time and options.

"Rayna always had a flair for theatrics. She likes to reveal things in her own time, in her own way." Emily opened a vintage copy of 'Pride and Prejudice,' and pretended to read, clearly trying to change the subject.

Rayna returned, her footsteps silent as she walked through the kitchen wall. Her eyes flitted towards the ground, a faint blush rising on her cheeks before she raised her chin and adopted a haughty demeanor. "All right then," she said slowly, crossing her arms as if to prove a point. "Where were we?"

"We were at the part where you withheld important information about your rivalry with Olivia and then vanished," I snapped.

Rayna sighed, her icy demeanor slipping for just a second. "Fine, listen. Olivia and I had our differences, yes. But, when you've been in this cutthroat industry long enough, you learn to keep your enemies close. That's all I'm saying."

"And what about Blake?" I pressed. "Did you ever confront Olivia about your relationship with him?"

Rayna's eyes flickered as if she was juggling fiery torches of emotion. "Are you kidding? Olivia was the kind of woman who never looked over her shoulder. She walked off that runway and right into high society like she was born wearing pearls."

"That doesn't answer my question. Did you tell her you were having an affair with Blake?"

Rayna's icy façade cracked just a smidgen. "No, I didn't. But believe me, Olivia found her own catwalk in high society, her own spotlight. She didn't need Blake—or the fashion world—to define her."

"So she left that world entirely when she married Blake?"

"Yes, and with the grace of a seasoned performer, too. In many ways, she got her happy ending. She didn't need the industry to define her," she repeated.

"So Olivia wasn't as clueless as everyone thought," I mused, feeling the weight of my recent discoveries.

Rayna's spectral form shimmered as if responding to a chill. "Olivia had her own playbook, darling. She always did."

"Did you know she hired a PI to tail Blake? To keep tabs on his, let's say, extracurricular activities?"

Rayna let out a hollow chuckle. "That's rich. No, I didn't know. But it doesn't surprise me. Olivia might have been many things, but blind was not one of them."

"I wonder if Blake knew he was being watched. Did he ever act like he suspected his secret outings were not-so-secret?"

Rayna's eyes, still the same stormy blue, narrowed. "Blake might have had his flaws, but being a novice at deception wasn't among them. If he suspected, he never let on—especially not to me."

"You sound almost... respectful," I said, my words laced with surprise.

Rayna's eyes met mine, locking in like two snipers taking aim. "I never agreed with Olivia's life choices, but I do respect her ability to change the game, to rewrite the rules. She was once 'queen of the runway,' and then she became the queen of something entirely different."

"So, the tension between you two was—?"

Rayna cut me off with a chuckle that was colder than a witch's brew. "Pure, unfiltered jealousy? Please, we were more complex than that. She had Blake, sure, and I wanted him. In our world, jealousy is far too simplistic. Let's just say we had different scripts, different stages, and different roles to play. My affair with Blake was just one of the scenes."

My phone buzzed. Seb was checking in: "Audrey, you better be Zen!"

I quickly texted back, "Couldn't be any Zener."

Shoving my phone into my pocket, I felt around for my keys. "Uh oh."

Emily closed the book she'd been pretending to read. "What's up?"

"My keys. I left them next door."

Ben barked out a laugh. "Of course you did."

"Not helpful, Benjamin," I said jokingly, giving him a warm smile to show I was teasing. We were so close to breaking the case; I just needed solid evidence or a confession from Olivia, and it would all be wrapped up in a pretty red bow, and Rayna could cross over. With any luck, Leo would make progress on Emily's case, and I'd get a two-for-one deal. All I needed was my keys and my car, and I was good to go.

"Can you guys keep a lookout for me while I sneak next door? Seb cannot know about this."

"Ah, a clandestine operation. How thrilling!" Emily's eyes twinkled with excitement. "We're your ghostly surveillance team!"

"Okay, Audrey, you got this," I muttered to myself as I peered out of Seb's dining-room window. My cheek pressed against the cool glass as I attempted to look into my backyard while hiding from prying eyes. My house was bursting with activity, with decorators, florists, and what seemed like a small army of wedding planners buzzing around. Seb was directing traffic, maneuvering a ridiculously large arch into the garden.

I tried to summon my inner 007 as I cracked open the back door. All was quiet as I slipped outside, and from here, the coast looked clear.

Ben returned from a reconnaissance next door. "Okay, Seb's busy arguing with a florist about peonies. Now's your chance."

My heart raced as I scurried across the lawn and slipped through the side gate. I felt like a cat burglar in my own home, sneaking past the windows as I made my way to the back door.

I was about to take my first step onto the back deck when Emily hissed, "Stop! Seb is coming!" I ducked behind a bush without hesitation and watched Seb walk past me, carrying a box of twinkling fairy lights. He placed them on the deck before he called out something to someone across the garden, hurrying toward them, waving his clipboard. "Quickly!" Emily whispered urgently. "Go now!"

I bolted through the back door and into the kitchen, grabbing my keys from the counter. I let out a sigh of relief; phase one complete. Now for the escape.

Crouching low, I made a beeline for my garage. Holding my breath, I got into the car, started the engine, and eased it out as quietly as one could ease out a running SUV. Only then did I allow myself to breathe again.

"Mission accomplished," Ben appeared next to me, giving me a ghostly high-five as I drove off.

I grinned, my heart still racing. "I owe you big time." Noticing we were down a couple of ghosts, I asked, "Rayna and Emily?"

"Distracted by all the shiny, pretty things happening at your place."

"Actually, that's probably for the best. Less of a distraction with those two running commentary on everything, although I would have thought Rayna would have come, at least to hear what Blake has to say."

"Maybe she already knows what he's going to say and doesn't want to hear it?" Ben suggested. "Pretty sure she's done her fair share of stalking him since she's been on this side of the living."

"Oh," poor Rayna. I figured maybe she'd seen or heard things that opened her eyes to the man Blake really was, and that had to hurt.

My car rolled up the long driveway, crunching on gravel as it came to a stop. The sprawling mansion loomed before me, its enormous oak door standing sentinel. Taking a deep breath, I grabbed my purse and stepped out of the car, feeling the warm sun on my skin.

My steps felt heavy as I walked closer, my heart thumping in my chest. Even though Blake had an alibi, something about him—and Olivia—still didn't sit right with me. When I reached the door, I pressed the bell and heard its metallic chime echo throughout the house. A minute passed before Olivia opened the door, her eyes widening in surprise.

"Audrey? Again? To what do I owe the pleasure?" Her words dripped with insincerity as she swept an arm invitingly toward the grand foyer. She didn't mention her earlier visit, and neither did I.

Stepping inside, I glanced around the marbled hall. "I wanted to talk to you and Blake. Is he home?"

Olivia hesitated for a fraction of a second. "He's in his study. But I'm not sure he has time for... unexpected visits."

"I'll take my chances."

As Olivia led me through the maze of opulence, I couldn't help but notice the walls adorned with photographs. Then, one photograph caught my attention—it wasn't just a picture; it was an era. A much younger Olivia was captured mid-stride on a runway, commanding it as if it were a kingdom. She wore a sleek, midnight-blue gown that clung to her like a second skin, its fabric shimmering as though sprinkled with stardust. Her eyes weren't just looking forward; they were challenging the future. The flashing bulbs of the cameras and the blurry outlines of the audience framed her, but she was the epicenter, the star around which everything else orbited.

"Is this from your modeling days?" I inquired, my eyes narrowing at the photograph.

Olivia paused, looking at the photo as if seeing it for the first time. "Ah, yes. Seems like a lifetime ago."

"You look so different. Was it before you married Blake?"

She nodded, her gaze lingering on the photo. "It was a different world, a different life. But, let's not dwell on the past."

Curious but deciding not to push for now, I followed her down the corridor until we reached a heavy wooden door. She pushed open the door without knocking.

"Blake, you have a visitor."

Blake looked up from his desk, a sea of papers and an open laptop before him. His eyes widened as he saw me.

"Audrey. This is bordering on harassment."

"I like to keep people on their toes," I retorted, feeling the tension in the room build.

Olivia excused herself, saying she'd let us talk. But as she left the room, she gave me a look that was hard to decipher—a cocktail of curiosity, skepticism, and a hint of apprehension.

Blake leaned back in his leather chair. "So, what do you want?"

"I would have thought that was obvious."

Blake's gaze hardened. "If you're here about Rayna, I've already told you. I have an alibi."

"Alibis can be arranged."

"And hitmen can be hired," he retorted, raising an eyebrow.

I felt my pulse quicken. He was challenging me, almost daring me to accuse him.

"I'm not here to play games, Blake. I'm here to find out who killed Rayna. Whether it's you, Olivia, or someone else entirely."

"Is that so?" Blake circled around his desk, coming to stand just a few feet from me. "And why would Olivia ever harm Rayna?"

"Perhaps to save her marriage? Or maybe to reclaim her position as the true queen of this little empire you've built."

Blake chuckled, but there was no humor in his eyes. "Olivia doesn't need to reclaim anything. She's always been the queen. Rayna was merely... a distraction."

"A distraction you were willing to risk your marriage for?"

"A distraction that reminded me of my wife—when she was younger, less consumed by social circles and charity events," Blake shot back, his words tinged with a bitterness I hadn't detected before.

"But distractions can become threats, can't they?" I pressed.

His eyes locked onto mine, and in an instant, a chill ran down my spine. "Is that a question or an accusation?"

Before I could respond, the door creaked open, and Olivia walked in, holding a silver tray with a pot of tea and three cups. "I thought we could all use some refreshments."

As she set the tray down, Olivia met my eyes, and I knew it was time to cut through the B.S. "Olivia, can you explain why your phone pinged off a cell tower near the expo at the time of Rayna's death? The very time you said you weren't there?"

Her eyes tightened, a look of both surprise and irritation. "You're still probing into this? Haven't the police already cleared me?"

"They might have questioned you, but they haven't cleared you. Your alibi about being at a charity meeting is bogus. They haven't had a meeting in weeks."

Olivia's voice came out clipped. "Fine. I lost my phone a few days ago, okay? Happy now? This one," she pulled a cell phone from the pocket of her dress, "is new."

"Lost your phone?" I quirked an eyebrow. "That's convenient, given the circumstances. So, what's your real alibi, then?" As I leaned into my questioning, Ben whispered in my ear, "I'll take a look around the house, see if Olivia's hiding a second phone."

Olivia's face flushed with anger. "I've told the police everything. I'm getting my lawyer, and I'll be pressing charges against you for harassment."

With a calm steadiness, I said, "Involve your lawyer if you think that's best. But understand that the truth has a way of surfacing, Olivia. The secrets between you and Blake aren't just yours anymore. They're evidence."

Her eyes narrowed, clearly weighing her options. "You're playing with fire, Audrey."

"Sometimes, fire is the only way to see through the smoke," I replied, not backing down. "The clock's ticking for all of us. So where were you, really?"

Olivia sighed, her face a mix of aggravation and reluctant defeat. "Fine," she snapped, "if you must know, I was at my lawyer's office."

I raised an eyebrow. "Doing what? Getting advice on how to cover up a murder? Divorce papers, perhaps?"

Out of the corner of my eye, I saw Blake shift uncomfortably, his expression unreadable but taut like a pulled bowstring.

Olivia looked like she'd just bitten into a particularly unpleasant hors d'oeuvre. "You have quite a vivid imagination, Audrey. No, I was picking up a contract. A very lucrative modeling gig in Paris intended for Rayna."

My head snapped back. "You were what now?"

Blake let out a barely audible "Huh," as if this news was surprising but also perfectly on-brand for Olivia. His eyebrows lifted just a millimeter, his version of a jaw drop.

Olivia leaned in, voice low. "It was a deal. A way

to get Rayna out of our lives, out of Blake's life specifically. All she had to do was end the affair, move to Paris, and I'd make her career explode. My lawyer drew up an airtight agreement. If she backed out, I could crush her career like a grape."

Blake crossed his arms, nodding almost imperceptibly. Surprised but hardly surprised, it was as if he'd discovered a secret compartment in a drawer he'd been using for years.

She looked up, meeting my eyes. "I planned on presenting her with the contract the afternoon of the expo when she'd be riding high and most likely to take the bait."

I stared at her, speechless for a moment. "You were willing to pay her off to disappear?"

"I was willing to do whatever it took to save my marriage. Aside from murder, contrary to what you might think. Now you know. Is this alibi good enough for you, or should I fetch my attorney to make it official?"

"You know what they say, Olivia. Pics, or it didn't happen. Or, in this case, docs, or you're still a suspect."

Olivia's eyes narrowed at me, her mouth a tight line. "You want proof? Fine." With a theatrical sigh, she reached into her designer bag, producing a thick manila envelope. "Behold, the golden ticket that was supposed to make Rayna disappear."

She waved the envelope in the air, rustling the paper for dramatic effect before tossing it onto the coffee table.

"Feel free to read every clause, every stipulation," Olivia snapped, her eyes defiant. "It's as ironclad as they come."

Blake picked up the envelope, extracting a few pages and scanning them. His eyebrows performed that fractional lift again—a blend of surprise and that peculiar brand of *I-knew-it* satisfaction. He tossed the papers back onto the table, a wry smile tugging at the corners of his mouth.

"Looks legit," he muttered, settling back into his seat as if we'd just confirmed the sky was, indeed, blue.

I grabbed the contract and skimmed through it. The language was legalese-heavy, but the gist was clear: Rayna gets a new life in Paris if—and it was a big if—she cut all ties with Blake.

Olivia crossed her arms. "Satisfied, Audrey? Or would you like to call in a forensic team to verify the ink? Perhaps call my attorney to confirm I was, indeed, in his office at 2.30 p.m. the day of the expo." Pulling her phone out of her pocket, she opened her calendar app and held it out for me to see.

"See? Right there. Meeting at Beasley, Tate and Associates."

I cringed. It had to be the law firm Amanda worked at, didn't it?

"You could have entered that into your diary at any time," I pointed out.

"Think what you want, Audrey," Olivia retorted, her icy composure regaining ground. "I've given you the truth. Take it or leave it."

Ben returned, strolling through the wall. "She just might be telling the truth," he said. "I didn't find any second phones hidden away anywhere."

"Alibis are only as good as the paper they're written on. Hold tight."

Pulling out my phone, I scrolled for Amanda's number. Our relationship was as complex as a Rubik's Cube and equally colorful. One ring. Two rings.

"Hello, Audrey." Amanda's cultured tones filled my ear.

"Hey, Amanda. Listen, I need a favor."

"You never call me just to chat, do you? How's wedding preparations going?"

I rolled my eyes, glancing at Olivia, who was

tapping her foot impatiently. "Fantastic. I'm relaxing at Seb's house, face mask on, painting my toenails in blissful anticipation."

Amanda laughed, "Really? You? I hope you're not smudging the carpet."

"Perish the thought," I replied. "Look, I need you to check something for me. A client at your law firm, Olivia Kingston—yes, that Olivia—claims she was there the day of the expo at 2:30 p.m. to pick up a contract. Can you confirm?"

"Audrey, I wasn't even there! I was at the expo with you."

"I know, I know. But can you pull some strings? This is important."

Amanda sighed. "All right. Give me a moment."

I could hear the tapping of a keyboard, Amanda's voice muttering something to someone at the other end. Olivia's gaze was drilling holes into me. Blake looked like he was seeing his wife in a whole new light. One he found immensely appealing.

"Okay, I've got it," Amanda finally said. "Yes, Olivia had an appointment the day before yesterday at 2:30 p.m. with one of our senior partners. Is that what you needed?"

"Exactly. Thanks, Amanda. You're a lifesaver."

"Anytime," she said, her tone warming a smidge. "I'll see you this afternoon."

"Absolutely, see you then," I said before hanging up.

I turned to Olivia, meeting her eyes squarely. "Your story checks out." Nodding toward the tea tray, I said, "I'll skip on the tea."

"I'll see you out." I got the feeling Olivia wasn't offering out of politeness. She was making sure I left.

I was almost out the door when I paused, my eyes drifting back to that photograph of Olivia in her younger days—on the runway in that striking midnight-blue gown. The scene was a stark contrast to the reserved, tight-lipped woman standing before me.

"You never told me about the dress you were wearing in that photo," I said, turning back toward her. "It's stunning. Who's the designer?"

Olivia sighed, her eyes following mine to the photograph. "Marianne Thompson designed that dress. She was something of a rising star back then."

"Marianne Thompson, you say?" My eyes narrowed. "Funny, I heard she might be the blonde woman you argued with at the expo."

Olivia's eyes widened for just a moment, a chink

in her carefully constructed armor. "You're mistaken."

"Am I?" I shrugged. "Maybe, maybe not. But I'm pretty good at jigsaw puzzles, Olivia. And right now, you and Marianne are pieces that almost fit."

"Good luck with your wedding, Audrey," Olivia said, her words almost mocking as if she knew how preoccupied I was and how little I was thinking about the ceremony.

"Thank you," I said, my eyes locking onto the photograph on the wall one last time. Olivia, the young model. A detail I'd have to revisit.

I got into my car, the weight of Rayna's murder heavier than ever. My mind was a whirlpool of questions, none of which I had answers to.

As I drove away, my phone buzzed—Seb, asking where I was. Ignoring the call, my eyes flicked to the dashboard clock. Solving a murder still fits into the day's schedule. Wedding prep could wait. There was still time.

CHAPTER FIFTEEN

"*B*en, how did you get on chasing those threatening emails Marianne Thompson received?" I asked, glancing in my rearview mirror as the regal structures of the Kingston mansion shrank to a pinprick in the distance. Ben's forehead wrinkled in a silent curse as he ran a hand through his hair. "I can't believe I forgot to tell you," he said. "Get this— she set up a fake email account with a bogus name and then sent herself those threats."

My eyes widened in alarm, and I nearly veered off the road. "What?!" I exclaimed. "Good Lord, why would someone do that?"

"Publicity?" Ben suggested. "Make herself look like a victim."

"This is getting odder by the minute." As I approached the junction, I slowed my car to a halt and flicked on the indicator before turning left, making a beeline for Marianne's boutique.

The drive took no more than ten minutes before I found myself standing outside Eclat Designs. It appeared that Marianne was fabricating stories of being threatened. My curiosity was piqued—I had to know why she'd do such a thing.

I opened the door of the boutique, which announced my arrival with a gentle tinkle. Marianne was deeply focused on her sketchbook but lifted her eyes when I walked in, a bit startled.

"Audrey? What are you doing here?"

"Following a hunch," I replied.

As I scanned the room, my eyes landed on a framed photograph near Marianne's desk. It showed a younger Olivia on what was unmistakably a fashion runway. She looked every inch the professional model, glamorous and confident. What caught my eye was the gown she was wearing.

It looked eerily similar to the gown on one of Marianne's mannequins, a gown that bore an elegant sign stating it was her latest creation. Now, seeing Olivia in that gown, in a photograph that was obviously years old, I had to wonder. Was

Marianne's latest creation not as original as she claimed?

The pieces of the puzzle began fitting together in a rather unsettling way. Why hadn't I noticed this photograph yesterday when I was here? Then it hit me—yesterday, I didn't know Olivia had been a model. My eyes must have skimmed over the photo, dismissing it as irrelevant. But today, I was seeing it with fresh eyes, eyes that knew Olivia had once walked the runway.

"Interesting photo you've got here. Olivia looks stunning in that gown." My gaze shifted from the picture to Marianne, playing my cards close to my chest and not revealing everything yet.

She followed my gaze, her eyes narrowing as they settled on the photograph. "Oh, that old thing? Yes, Olivia was quite the show-stopper back then. The camera loved her."

"You designed that dress for her, didn't you?"

She hesitated, her eyes meeting mine. "Yes, I did. That was one of my early designs."

"So, you and Olivia go way back. Interesting how her old gown looks almost identical to your latest creation over there." I gestured toward the mannequin draped in the all-too-familiar midnight-blue gown.

Marianne's eyes flickered, a split-second of panic before her practiced smile returned. "Designs evolve, Audrey. Styles come back into vogue."

"Or get recycled?" I ventured, pushing the envelope.

She bristled at that, her lips tightening. "Are you suggesting something?"

"Me? No, I'm just trying to understand why you would go through the trouble of sending yourself threatening emails, and now I find out you and Olivia share a... let's call it a tangled past."

Marianne's eyes darted around the room as if looking for an escape. Finally, she sighed. "Fine. I sent those emails to myself. Business has been slow, and a little publicity never hurt anyone."

"But plagiarizing an old design? How does that figure into your plan?"

Marianne stared at the photo, her eyes misty with a cocktail of nostalgia and regret. She finally turned to me. "You see that dress Olivia is wearing? I designed it. But let's just say Olivia became the headline, and the dress became a footnote. My work was eclipsed by her star power."

I cocked my head, absorbing the bitterness in her tone. "So, what you're saying is that Olivia upstaged you. But this gown"—I gestured toward the mannequin wearing either an identical or very similar dress to the one in the photograph—"is your mic drop, your unmissable soliloquy?"

Her eyes ignited, a spark long buried beneath years of being overlooked. "Exactly. It's time the spotlight landed where it always should have—on the real talent."

"So, it's safe to say you'd do anything to protect this design, your golden ticket back into the world of haute couture?"

Marianne's lips tightened. "Well, I wouldn't go that far."

But something in her eyes told me she'd already gone much farther than she'd ever admit.

The air between us grew thick like we were both walking through a mist of unspoken truths. "You know, plagiarism is the curse of the creative world. Designs, ideas, they're all vulnerable."

Marianne's gaze sharpened, a hint of anxiety creeping in. "What are you insinuating?"

"Me? Nothing," I said, my tone innocent. "I'm just commenting on how hard it must be to make something original these days. Like that gown, Emily was modeling, or the one Rayna wore—both exceptional pieces, and everyone's talking about them."

Her hands clenched at her sides, a bead of sweat appearing on her brow. "Why are you bringing them up?"

"Just making conversation," I shrugged. "But speaking of Rayna and Emily, it's interesting that both of them died while wearing your designs. Any thoughts on that?"

Marianne took a shaky breath, her veneer cracking just a little. "It's a horrifying coincidence, nothing more."

I smiled, but it didn't reach my eyes. "Coincidences make for good fiction, Marianne, but they're hard to swallow in real life. Especially for someone like me, who tends to question everything."

"As you should," she retorted, her voice tinged with defensiveness. "But I have nothing to hide."

I stepped closer, locking eyes with her. "Let's hope for your sake that's true. Because when it comes to digging for the truth, I'm relentless."

As I headed towards the door, my gaze paused on the picture of Olivia. "It's funny how a single photo can start unraveling a lifetime of lies."

After leaving Eclat Designs, my thoughts were racing like a greyhound after a rabbit. I needed more information, and there was one person who could help me connect the dots—Leo. As much as I didn't want to spill all my cards to the investigative reporter, his insight could be invaluable.

I parked outside the offices of the "Firefly Gazette," where Leo worked. The atmosphere was always lively here, with employees buzzing around in a flurry. It was like a beehive full of caffeine-fueled energy, gossip, and politics.

Entering Leo's office, I was immediately met by the chaos of papers scattered across his desk and empty coffee cups. Leo was squinting at his laptop, frantically typing with the ferocity of a cat hunting a laser point.

"Ah, Audrey, come in! Have a seat," he gestured to an empty chair buried under a mountain of research—newspapers, photographs, old notebooks. He moved the mess aside with a single sweep of his arm.

"Been busy, I see."

"Immensely. I've been interviewing everyone who was present at the mansion on the day Emily was killed. And let me tell you, that list is longer than my last relationship."

"Any luck?" I asked, my eyes darting to the laptop screen. It was filled with notes in a font so small it would make a magnifying glass cry.

"A bit. Several inconsistencies, unverified alibis, the usual. But something interesting—apparently, Emily made a comment about the gown she was wearing during the photo shoot."

"Oh?" I tilted my head, all ears but keeping my poker face intact.

"Yeah," Leo scratched his head, "Someone overheard her saying she was surprised the gown was a Marianne Thompson design. Said it reminded her of a gown by some other designer ... what was it... ah, yes, Vincente Gerardo. She seemed genuinely surprised. Now, why would she say that?"

The breadcrumb. I felt my pulse quicken, but I played it cool. "Maybe she was just being conversational? Sometimes models do chit-chat to pass the time."

"Could be," he said, "but Emily was known to have a keen eye for fashion. She wouldn't mistake a Chanel for a Walmart if you get what I mean."

"True. So, what's the plan now?"

"I'm digging deeper into everyone's background. I want to know who had the motive and opportunity. George Dawson's still a suspect, but he's disappeared. It's like chasing a ghost."

I nodded, pondering my next move. "Maybe you could look into that gown angle a bit more. If Emily was last seen in it, it might be a significant clue. Perhaps trace the lineage of that particular design?"

Leo looked intrigued. "Good point. Maybe there's more to that gown than just fabric and thread. It could tell us who had a reason to shut Emily up for good."

"I wouldn't put it past anyone in the high-stakes world of fashion," I said. But as I spoke, the voice in the back of my head was screaming Marianne's name.

"I'll get on it," Leo said, already lost in another tab on his computer.

"I'll dig up some past designs of Marianne's, see if there's a pattern to her, uh, creative inspiration. Any chance you've got a spare desk and laptop I could use?" I was on a time crunch. It made sense to do what I needed to do here.

"Sure, I can set you up. There's an empty desk right over there. Let me grab you a laptop."

I followed him into the open office space, the newsroom humming softly in the background, clacking keyboards and ringing phones—a soothing rhythm to the chaos that is small-town journalism.

"Sorry about the mess," he said, clearing some papers and handing me a laptop. "Let's call this your temporary HQ."

"Just like old times," I smirked. Before taking over Delaney Investigations, I'd been an office temp, and I'd had an assignment or two at the paper. I opened the laptop and got straight to it. I needed to dig up Marianne's past designs and see if they were knock-offs, bootlegs, or just overpriced déjà vu.

Leo hovered over my shoulder. "So, what's the plan?"

"Checking out Marianne's previous designs," I replied, my fingers flying over the keyboard. Her plagiarism was still a hunch. I needed proof.

"Okay, well, I'll leave you to it." Leo sauntered away, but not without a long lingering glance at my laptop screen. While I needed his help, I didn't want him to swoop in and steal the story—not until I'd solved the crime. Then, it was all his.

Picking up my phone, I fake-called Ben, who'd been following me around since we left the Kingston's.

"Ben?" I said into the phone, getting his attention from where he was reading the staff notice board across the room. He turned his head and mouthed, 'Me?' I nodded. Making his way over to my temporary desk, he leaned against it, half sinking through it so the wooden top dissected his midsection. "What do you need?"

"Can you interview Emily and Rayna? Ask about Marianne. Rumors, innuendos, anything."

"On it." He disappeared, and I put down my phone.

"Leo?" I called, leaning back in my chair.

"Yeah," he yelled from his office.

"Ever heard of a fashion historian?"

"You mean like an Indiana Jones for frocks?"

I chuckled, standing and crossing to lean against the doorframe of his office. "Sort of. Someone who knows the history of fashion, back to its buttonless origins. I've got to authenticate some designs here."

Leo flipped open his Rolodex. Yes, a Rolodex. Even in this digital age, the man was old-school and proud of it. "Ah, here we go. A professor at the local community college. She's written papers on fashion history. Will that work?"

"Perfect," I replied, grabbing the number.

Minutes later, I was chatting with a bona fide fashion historian. She agreed to examine the designs and offer her opinion. One step closer to knowing if Marianne was just a creative borrower or a stone-cold plagiarist.

As I hung up, Leo raised an eyebrow. "Well, you're certainly drilling down into this one. Feel like sharing what you've found?"

"Let's just say, in fashion, one day you're in, and the next day you're out," I replied. "And Marianne? She might just be on her way out."

I turned my attention to the screen and began trawling through archives, looking for any evidence of Marianne's prior "inspirations."

I could hear Leo in his office, engrossed in phone interviews, and I caught snippets of conversations. It was like listening to an audiobook you were dying to finish but had to wait for the next chapter to load.

I really wasn't expecting to hear from the fashion historian anytime soon, so when her number flashed on my screen with an incoming text, I was pleasantly surprised. Swiping open the message, my eyes scanned the text. It read, "*Marianne has been suspected of copying designs early in her career. Though nothing was proven, she had a feud with another designer, Viktor Ivanov, who accused her of plagiarism. The case was settled out of court.*"

"Score," I whispered under my breath. A settled court case wasn't an admission of guilt, but it wasn't a gold star for integrity, either.

CHAPTER SIXTEEN

*S*uddenly, Ben appeared right beside me, startling me so much that I almost lost my balance and toppled out of my seat. "Whoa, Ben! You gotta stop doing that. I swear, you're gonna give me a heart attack, and then I'll be one of you!"

He chuckled. "Emily and Rayna have some interesting tidbits about Marianne. Want me to bring them here?"

I eyed Leo, who was engrossed in a call, phone glued to his ear while scribbling so furiously you'd think he was drafting the constitution of his own secret society. Summoning ghosts to the Gazette office was risky. "No, let's not draw any more attention to ourselves," I whispered. "I'll meet you at Seb's house."

I grabbed my purse, logged out of the laptop, and stood up. "Leo, I have to jet, but keep me posted on any developments, okay?"

He nodded, scribbling something down even as he said his goodbyes to the person on the other end of the line. "Will do, Audrey. I feel like we're circling in on something big here."

"We're so close I can practically smell the ink drying on the front-page exposé," I quipped as I left the office, heading for Seb's house.

I'd just climbed into my car, tossed my bag on the passenger seat, and clicked my seat belt on when I saw something I was definitely not expecting to see. Marianne's face was reflected in my rearview mirror, hiding in the back seat of my car.

My gaze locked onto the mirror—there it was, a gun leveled at me. The very weapon, I was certain, that had ended Emily and Rayna. "Going somewhere, Audrey?" Marianne's voice dripped with malice.

My heart hammered in my chest like a drum, each beat echoing a countdown to an unknown fate. My spine went rigid as if jolted by a bolt of lightning, every nerve ending buzzing with electric dread. A warm sensation trickled down my leg, and oh boy, I'm pretty sure that's not my mocha latte. I've just peed a little, and I can't help but think, "Fantastic, my obituary is going to include the phrase 'died with wet pants.'"

"What do you want, Marianne?" I asked, trying to keep my voice steady as if I hadn't just turned my jeans into a mini-wading pool.

"What do you think? You're meddling in affairs that don't concern you. I intend to put a stop to it," she snarled.

"Killing me won't erase your past or cover up your lies."

"But it will silence you. Drive," Marianne commanded, aiming the gun at my head. "Head to Crystal Lake Road. Don't try anything funny, or I'll shoot."

I gripped the wheel, glancing at my phone in the passenger seat. There was no way to dial 911 without her noticing. Starting the car, I pulled out onto the road, my mind racing as fast as my heart, pondering how I ended up with a one-way ticket to Murder Town.

"Going for a swim, are we?" I asked jovially, trying to keep my voice light, yet all I could think of was that gun and the dark water at Crystal Lake. Oh, and the minor bladder leak, but priorities, right?

"Just shut up and drive."

My grip tightened on the wheel until my knuckles turned white, each mile clicking away like seconds while I frantically tried to come up with an escape plan that involved me not being shot. My purse sits on the passenger seat, my phone inside, tantalizingly close but unreachable.

We pass a sign that reads "Crystal Lake Road, 2 miles." I flashback to every action movie I've ever seen. What would Bruce Willis do? A voice in my head suggests calling her "Yippee-ki-yay," but I dismiss it as absurdly unhelpful. And yet, even action heroes can have weak bladders. A slight warm dampness reminds me that courage and a solid pelvic floor don't always go hand-in-hand.

"You're making a huge mistake, Marianne," I said, doing my best to hide the panic in my voice. I took a deep breath, desperately trying to appear cool and unflappable—very un-peed-in-pants-like. "Why all the cloak-and-dagger stuff? If you're so eager to chat, you could've just sent a text. Oh wait, you did!"

Marianne's eyes narrowed. "So, you got my little messages. Shame you didn't take the hint and back off."

"So you *are* the mystery texter. Funny, most people just say, 'We need to talk,' not resort to attempted murder. But then again, you've always been a 'go big or go home' kinda gal."

Marianne's grip tightened around the gun. "Drive faster. We're almost there."

My heart skipped a beat as I saw another sign for Crystal Lake. "You know, if you shoot me, you're never going to clear your name. Is that what you want? To always be on the run?"

Marianne hesitated, the gun wavering slightly. "You don't understand. You can't possibly fathom the pressure I'm under."

"Oh, enlighten me," I urged, catching her eyes in the rearview mirror.

She sighed deeply. "Fine. I'll indulge you. Pretty sure, given time, you'd have worked it out for yourself, anyway. It all comes down to Olivia Kingston."

I stiffened. "Olivia? How?"

"Years ago, I borrowed a design from Viktor Ivanov. Olivia was modeling it. When Viktor threatened to sue, Olivia paid him off to keep her name out of it. Even then, she was all about protecting *her* name, *her* reputation."

Suddenly, the pieces fell into place. "So that's your connection to her? A buried secret?"

Marianne's eyes clouded with a mix of

resentment and regret. "Olivia got wind I might be, let's say, 'recycling' designs again. She was livid. Told me she saved my skin once by buying off that other designer—not for my sake, mind you, but to protect her own sparkling reputation. She warned me there'd be no second act of mercy."

I raised an eyebrow. "And if the truth about her earlier bailout gets out?"

Marianne's voice quivered. "She promised something far worse than legal action. She threatened to destroy me in the industry to make sure no one would touch my designs with a ten-foot pole. Olivia has contacts influence; she could make it happen."

"So that was you, in the CCTV footage, arguing with Olivia at the expo?" I asked, my eyes narrowing.

Marianne exhaled, her shoulders drooping ever so slightly. "She and I have had several 'come-to-Jesus' talks about my 'creative inspirations.' Each conversation was more chilling than the last. This last warning was clear—no more chances. It was her final ultimatum."

I eyed Marianne skeptically. "So what you're saying is, you've basically been walking on a tightrope of Olivia's making. One false move, and you plummet."

She nodded, eyes narrowing. "Exactly. Olivia holds the net, and she's not afraid to yank it away. I've been living on borrowed time and borrowed... well, other things."

Marianne leaned forward, her eyes now gleaming with a cunning light. "During one of those 'friendly warnings' she was so fond of giving, Olivia got so heated she stormed out and left her phone behind. A minor oversight that gave me an idea."

I was pretty sure I knew where this was going. "Go on."

Smirking, Marianne continued, "I didn't just keep Olivia's phone; I used a burner to send some rather incriminating texts. You know, to make it look like she was the mastermind behind all of this. So when the expo came along, voilà! I saw my opening for a bit of poetic justice. I planted Olivia's phone there, like a delicious breadcrumb that would lead the hungry hounds straight to her and turn the spotlight away from me."

"So, you frame Olivia, kill me, and then what? Live happily ever after?"

Marianne's eyes looked wild, almost desperate. "I don't have any other choice!"

"Everyone has a choice, Marianne. The question is, are you making the right one?"

"Where the hell are you? You were supposed to be at Seb's house, like, ten minutes ago!" Ben popped into existence in the passenger seat, confusion and concern splashed across his face.

I shot him a panicked glance, trying not to alert Marianne. "I'm a little tied up right now." I hissed, jerking my head toward the unwelcome passenger in the back seat.

"Well, that escalated quickly," Ben muttered, swiveling to assess the situation.

"Any ideas how to get out of it?"

"Give me a minute."

Marianne's head snaps toward me. "Who are you talking to?" she snarled, pulling my seatbelt with a jerk that practically choked me.

My fingers scramble to loosen the seatbelt from my neck. "Hey!" I protested, "That hurts. What are you trying to do, kill us both?"

Ben twisted in his seat, his hands diving toward Marianne in a futile attempt to push her away. His hands passed right through her. "Bollocks," he muttered, sinking back into his seat. Then he sat bolt upright as if a spectral lightbulb had just lit up over his head. "I can text Kade—"

"Do it!"

In a nanosecond that felt like an eternity, my

phone pings—a message sent. "Done. I've told him you're hanging by a thread and pinged your location to him."

I sucked in a shaky breath as a road sign whizzed by: "Crystal Lake, 1 mile."

"Ah, the dreaded Crystal Lake," Ben states, his eyes widening at the sign. "You know, in any other context, it sounds like a charming vacation spot."

"You're not helping!" I snap, already crafting a high-risk plan in my mind.

Ben catches my expression. "You've got that 'Audrey's up to something' look."

"If she reaches that lake, I'm fish food," I whisper, but a plan is forming. It was not the smartest plan, possibly not the best plan, but it was a plan.

Marianne is not buckled in. I am. In a flash of grim realization, I understand what I must do. I gripped the wheel until my knuckles turned white. "Hold on to something, Ben. Things are about to get bumpy."

He grinned despite the circumstances. "Oh, this is going to be a tale for my best man's speech."

Marianne's eyes narrow. "What are you—"

That's my cue. I slammed my foot on the accelerator, and her unfinished question was swallowed by her own scream. The tires screech, throwing us around like we're dice in a Yahtzee cup as we careen into a sharp bend.

"Let's see how you like this turn of events!" I barely manage to bite back a shriek as the car spirals, the tail end fishtailing while tires spin, trying to find purchase on the asphalt. Time slows. It's like we're in a Matrix movie, only less cool and more terrifying.

CRASH.

We plowed into a tree, our forward momentum arrested by splintering wood and airbags. The windshield held its form, thanks to safety glass, but the web of cracks that appeared made it look like a piece of abstract art in a modern museum. The car made a choked noise, its engine sputtering as if gasping for air.

For a split second, we're motionless, caught in a snapshot of sheer terror and disbelief. Then adrenaline kicks my butt into gear. I shove open my jammed door and roll out, my legs wobbling like a newborn fawn's.

Behind me, Marianne's door creaks open. I twist around, and there she is: blood trickling down her face, pointing a gun at me. My eyes flick from the gun Marianne's brandishing to my purse flung from the car during our wild crash. It's lying in the grass a few feet away. Inside that bag is my taser—the closest thing to a fighting chance I've got against a loaded gun.

"Freeze," Marianne seethes, her voice tinged with pain. She's wobbly on her legs, clearly disoriented from the crash, but her eyes lock onto my desperate gaze toward the purse. Her faltering stance gives me a flicker of hope; maybe, just maybe, I have a fighting chance here.

"What, like 'Red Light, Green Light'?" I volley back, my eyes riveted on my purse. "Can I wiggle my nose? Is eyebrow movement allowed?"

Ignoring my barbs, Marianne lunged forward, gun still aimed at me. It's now or never. I leap, diving for my purse and ripping out my pink taser.

Marianne yelped a curse, losing her footing, her gun tumbling from her grip like it was done with this drama. I strike, jamming the taser into her side.

"Time for some shock and awe," I zing, pressing the trigger. The taser emits a sound like an angry bee on steroids. Marianne's body jerks, a one-woman dance-off from hell, before she crumples onto the grass, groaning.

Tires screech. Kade's car skids to a halt, his face a kaleidoscope of horror, relief, and 'what the hell just happened?' My legs go limp, gravity taking over as I sag to my knees.

As Kade sprints to my side and distant sirens howl their approach, I feel a myriad of things—relief, exhaustion, and, yeah, a bit of pee.

But most of all, I feel alive.

CHAPTER SEVENTEEN

In Detective McClain's office, I sat fidgeting on a chair that could have been the cousin of a Brillo pad. I tugged at my t-shirt, a grim testament to my tussle with Marianne. Kade was next to me, his hand a warm and steady weight on my knee. "Don't worry, it's just a formality," he'd whispered earlier. "We'll be out of here before you know it."

The door swung open, and in walked Detective McClain. If his face was a weather report, it'd read 'tired with a chance of smiles.'

"Audrey, Kade, I hear you've had an eventful afternoon."

"Thanks for taking over the case, Neal," Kade said. "As you know, I'm officially off duty, and our wedding is—" he glanced at his watch, "—closer than I'd care to admit."

McClain chuckled. "Ah, weddings. A deadline like no other. Thompson has confessed to everything—the murders, the kidnapping, the design theft."

I sat up, captivated. "She killed Emily because of the stolen bridal gown design?"

"Exactly. Emily got wind of the plagiarism and confronted her. Marianne saw red and painted the scene with it. Then she tried to frame George Dawson," he explained, punctuating his sentence with an eyebrow raise. "Turns out George had let slip that he was leaving the country, going to live in Bali. Marianne used that to her advantage, essentially casting suspicion that he was behind Emily's death."

"And it didn't end there," Kade chimed in. "Marianne silenced Rayna because she thought Rayna was onto her design theft, too."

"Yes, it appears that way," McClain confirmed, shuffling his paperwork. "The kicker? Rayna wasn't even aware of Marianne's stolen designs. She was a model, for heaven's sake, not an investigative journalist. Marianne killed her based on an erroneous assumption. Thought she was a threat when she was nothing of the sort."

Kade shook his head. "Wow, talk about jumping the gun—no pun intended."

"Exactly," I chimed in. "She silenced someone who was as clueless about her schemes as anyone. It's not just tragic, it's senseless."

"Her paranoia became her downfall. It's like she was weaving this intricate tapestry of deceit and ended up tangling herself in it." McClain picked up a pen, tapping it against the open file on his desk. "We won't keep you long, especially considering your, ahem, upcoming event," he said, glancing at his watch. "Just some final details. Olivia Kingston came in earlier. Voluntarily, mind you. Gave up her alibi for the time Rayna died. Seems she was visiting with her lawyer. Don't know why she wouldn't tell you that earlier when you brought her in for questioning," he shrugged. "Maybe she had a change of conscience. She's spilled the beans on her husband's affair with Rayna."

My eyes shot to Kade. "Why would she do that?"

Neal shrugged. "After her run-in with Marianne at the expo, Olivia decided to control the narrative. If the affair would come out anyway, better from her lips than the police blotter."

I sighed, a sense of icy disbelief coursing through me. Marianne's spiderweb of deceit had been intricate, but it had unraveled. Thanks to us.

"Okay, you lovebirds are free to go. Off with you," Neal said, waving us out of his office.

As we stepped out, the weight of the day settled on me, but the promise of tying the knot with Kade lightened my spirit. "We've got a wedding to get to," I said, smiling at him.

With sunbeams tiptoeing through the gauzy curtains, the atmosphere in Seb's living room could've been described as 'tranquil.' But when the ghosts of two murder victims surround you, tranquility goes out the window faster than Marianne's fashion career.

"So, you're saying Marianne killed us because her creativity was as real as a three-dollar bill?" Rayna sat in an armchair, the skirts from the gold gown enveloping her, looking more intrigued than vengeful.

"Yep, she was about as original as a Xerox machine," I confirmed, eyes darting between Rayna and Emily. "Even tried to use Olivia's marital drama to cover her tracks. Clever and dastardly. A toxic cocktail."

Rayna heaved a sigh, then waved a hand as if the whole big revelation of who killed them was yesterday's news. "Well, if I had to be offed, I'm glad it was for high-stakes drama and not some petty nonsense."

Emily tilted her spectral head. "Honey, I've been dead longer, and all I care about now is whether Audrey here will trip in her wedding heels."

Rayna's eyes twinkled. "Oh, I want front-row seats to that!"

I chuckled. "Trust me, you'll have the best seats in the house. The ethereal plane, or whatever we're calling it these days."

I grinned, but my eyes had that 'we-need-to-talk' seriousness as I leveled my gaze at the two ghostly models. "So, um, speaking of the ethereal plane, now that we've solved your murders—no applause necessary, but you're welcome—aren't you two due for a little trip? As in crossing over to the other side?"

Both women exchanged glances that suggested they hadn't packed their bags yet.

Emily folded her arms, her eyes filled with curiosity. "Is that how it works? We're suddenly enlightened, and—poof—we disappear into the light?"

"Um, usually? It's not my first ghost rodeo," I said, feeling the weight of those countless murder-solving hours. "I mean, your unfinished business here should be pretty much, well, finished, right?"

Rayna looked thoughtful. "You know, eternity's a long time. We might need another moment to savor our final mortal moments. Plus, I need to see if you trip on your way down the aisle."

"You two can't stick around forever," I cautioned. "It sort of defeats the purpose. The living need to live, and the dead... well, you can do whatever fabulous things await you on the other side."

Emily nodded slowly. "It's just, it's such a big step, Audrey. We're getting used to the idea. Thanks to you, we know what happened to us, and that's huge."

"Take your time," I offered in a softer tone, "but not too much time. I have wedding jitters, and a haunting is the last thing I need right now."

Rayna lifted her hands in mock surrender. "Don't worry, darling. When it's time, it'll be lights, camera, and ascension!"

I laughed, "All right, just remember, no haunting my honeymoon, capiche?"

"Deal," both women chimed in unison. A wave of warm fuzziness washed over me despite their belonging to the chillier side of existence.

The back door slammed open, and Seb came bounding in. How he had so much energy after spending virtually all day prepping for my wedding was beyond me.

"Audrey, the CWA Angels have outdone themselves. You like deviled eggs? We've got deviled eggs coming out of our ears!"

"Errr. Good to know."

Seb's eyes nearly popped out of his head as he took in the frazzled spectacle that was yours truly. "Sweet mercy, sugar, you look like you've tangled with a wind tunnel!"

Self-consciously, I ran my fingers through my hair, dislodging a twig. "You don't even know the half of it, Seb. I've been sleuthing, okay?"

He clasped his clipboard to his chest, aghast. "Clearly, honey, but even Miss Marple took time for a wash and set."

I glanced down at my dirt-smeared t-shirt. "Yeah, well, Miss Marple didn't have to deal with homicidal designers and impromptu country drives."

Seb flicked his pen over the clipboard, scrutinizing the timeline for my impending nuptials.

"All right, sugar, recalibrating. You've got a luxurious two to three hours to get yourself from 'who-done-it' to 'I-do.'"

I exhaled a sigh that felt like it had been building since Emily and Rayna first appeared in my life. "You mean I have time to actually breathe? Maybe even lay horizontal for a bit?"

Seb's eyebrows did a quick cha-cha up his forehead. "Honey, you've got time to not only lay down but to actually close your eyes. We might even be able to smuggle in a face mask and a cucumber slice or two!" Then he clapped his hands twice. "Okay, to all the ghosts in this room, I need you to give the girl a break. She needs her rest, and if you can see her face, I'm sure you'll agree with me."

Rayna raised a brow. "He can see us?"

I shook my head. "Nah. Seb can sense when you are around but can't see or hear you."

"Who's here?" Seb asked, used to me conversing with the undead in front of him.

"A couple of models, Rayna Mills and Emily Carson. But they should cross over soon since I sacrificed a good portion of my wedding day to solve their murders."

"Come on, Audrey, this is the fun part," Emily

urged, surging to her feet and pulling Rayna with her. "Isn't it Rayna?"

"Oh, it is," Rayna agreed. "The hair, the makeup..." they looked at each other, "the dress!" they said in unison.

"Wait, before I go," I paused at the threshold, spinning to face Emily and Rayna, "Promise me, no haunting antics during the ceremony? I don't want to say 'I do' and have you two scaring the confetti out of everyone."

Rayna grinned, "Darling if I wanted to make a scene, I would've done it years ago. Go, get hitched!"

Emily added, "Yeah, the only spirits I want involved in your wedding are the liquid kind. So, go already!"

Touched by their spectral excitement, I nodded. "Thanks. See you on the other side—of the ceremony that is."

As I walked across the front lawn, I could hear Seb talking to the ghosts he couldn't see or hear. "Rayna, Emily," his voice drifted from the open window. "Dolls. Would you be a couple of absolute angels and let Audrey get some rest? Lord almighty, but did you see the state of her?" his voice faded the further away I got. "I think Laura will need backup in the makeup department."

CHAPTER EIGHTEEN

I stumbled downstairs forty minutes later, rubbing my eyes and thinking about the hot cup of coffee that awaited me. Seb had cleared everyone out, and the house, alive earlier with the hustle and bustle of wedding preparations, was now blissfully silent. As I rounded the corner into the living room, my sleepy gaze landed on something that snapped me fully awake.

"Oh my God," I whispered, clutching my chest as if it could stop the impending heart attack.

There, where my beautiful Lise Magnier gown had been hanging so gracefully, was an unrecognizable mass of tulle, lace, and beaded fragments. The skirt looked as if a rabid animal had attacked it.

"Bandit!"

Speak of the devil. The little raccoon waddled out from behind the sofa, a pleased expression on her face, holding what looked like a shiny button in her tiny paws.

"Hey, Mom," she chirped, dropping the button at my feet as if presenting a treasure. "Look, I added a button. Now it's perfect!"

I looked from Bandit to the carnage that was once my wedding dress and back to Bandit. My eyes narrowed. "You think a button fixes this?"

Bandit looked puzzled, her head tilting to one side. "But it's a really nice button."

Thor padded into the room, surveying the destruction before commenting dryly, "Well, this is certainly one way to embrace the 'something borrowed, something ruined' tradition."

"Ruined is right," I moaned, sinking onto the sofa and staring at the remains of my wedding dress.

In the midst of my despair, I felt a tug on my sleeve. It was Bandit trying to console me. "I'm sorry, Mom. It's just... you and Mom Mom added something, and I wanted to add something, too. So it could be perfect."

I sighed, looking at the innocent eyes of my

mischievous raccoon. I couldn't stay mad at her. After all, she didn't know any better.

I picked up the button she'd presented me with and smiled faintly. "Thank you, Bandit. It's a very nice button."

I looked at the only part of the dress that remained intact—the bodice. "Well, it looks like I'm going to have a busy afternoon. A very, very busy afternoon."

And with that, I picked up my phone to make a frantic call. To Seb, of course. Who else could perform a wedding miracle on such short notice?

Seb arrived within minutes of my call, and when he walked in, his eyes went wide at the scene before him. "Oh, honey. This is... a situation."

"No kidding," I replied, gesturing to Bandit, who was now guiltily hiding behind the sofa.

Seb gave Bandit a sympathetic look. "Ah, the artist behind the masterpiece."

"If by masterpiece you mean disaster, then yes," I sighed.

"Don't you worry, darling. If anyone can turn this ship around, it's me. And I know just the crew to call." Seb whipped out his phone and began making a series of rapid-fire calls. Within minutes, his friends an entourage of fabulous drag queens, descended upon my house like a glam squad of fairy godmothers.

Mimi, a queen known for her sewing skills, took one look at the ruined dress and clapped her hands. "Darling, we're going to give this dress a resurrection worthy of a daytime soap opera comeback."

Stella, the makeup guru, started laying out an array of beauty products. "And we'll give you a look that's as show-stopping as the new dress."

Cherry, the wig specialist, simply said, "Trust me, we'll make your hair bigger than your problems today."

Time flew by in a whirl of laughter, storytelling, and more than a few tears—mostly mine, out of sheer gratitude. When they finally declared the dress complete, I looked in the full-length mirror and gasped. The dress was nothing short of a work of art. The original bodice remained intact, its beaded floral lace still sparkling, but from there, the creation took on a life of its own. Mimi had expertly woven layers upon layers of iridescent tulle in shades of blush pink, champagne, and the lightest whisper of lavender. It flowed into a full, voluminous skirt that glittered as if sprinkled with stardust.

The waist was cinched with an intricate rose-gold belt encrusted with Swarovski crystals, adding a regal touch. But it was the train that stole the show. Mimi had attached a detachable train made from cascading ruffles of multicolored tulle; each layer airbrushed with metallic hues to give a liquid metal effect. It was like a waterfall of rainbows flowing behind me. And amongst all that, a scrap of my grandmother's lace and Mom's button was rescued from Bandit.

Cherry, seizing the opportunity to further elevate the outfit, had added delicate strands of pearls and tiny LED lights within the layers of the train. Now, it didn't just flow; it glowed.

Not to be outdone, Stella had found a matching iridescent veil that shimmered in harmony with the train. It was like a fairy had spun her web of dreams into fabric.

Seb had placed the finishing touch: a tiara made of intertwined rose-gold and silver vines, dotted with pearls and tiny sapphires, which sat atop my head like a crown, making me feel like the queen of my own enchanted world.

The ensemble was outrageous, extraordinary, and utterly fabulous—each piece contributing to a symphony of color, light, and love. It wasn't just a dress; it was a statement, a story, a triumph. At that moment, looking at my reflection, I felt invincible, ready to take on whatever life—and love—had in store for me.

"Seb, I don't know how you pulled this off," I said, turning to my friend with misty eyes.

He put a finger to my lips. "Shush, darling. This is what we do. Turn tragedies into triumphs and messes into masterpieces."

Stella handed me a tissue. "Now, no more tears. You'll ruin your mascara."

As they helped me get ready, adding the final touches to my look, I realized that my wedding day, while not going according to the original plan, would be unique and filled with unexpected love. All thanks to a ruined dress, a raccoon with a penchant for buttons, and a group of drag queens who knew how to turn any situation fabulous.

"Seb," I whispered, still shocked at how utterly fabulous I looked. "You know, if Bandit hadn't confessed to her little alteration, I may have suspected it was you who'd sabotaged my dress just so you could have your wish come true and get me to not only wear a tiara with a veil but a train too. Seb, I'm going to break my neck!" My fears were not unfounded. My entire ensemble had the potential for disaster written all over it.

"Mimi, Cherry, Stella, gather around! Our bride

needs a quick tutorial," Seb announced, waving his flamboyant friends over.

Mimi stepped forward first, her six-inch stilettos clicking on the floor as she moved with surprising grace for someone in such towering footwear. "All right, darling, lesson number one: the train. It's long, so you'll need to lead with your hips, not your feet."

She demonstrated, swaying her hips exaggeratedly as she took small, deliberate steps. "See? You move from the waist, and the fabric follows. The key is to glide. Imagine you're floating on water."

Cherry chimed in next. "And, honey, don't just kick the train behind you. You need to be aware of it like it's an extension of you. If you don't respect the train, it'll trip you faster than a cat on a leash."

"Been there, done that," Stella added with a laugh as she approached and adjusted the veil and tiara. "Now, for these beauties. This veil is light, but it can catch on stuff if you're not careful. When you turn, make sure to lead with your shoulder like so," she demonstrated, making a slow, elegant turn, "so it naturally follows your movement without snagging on anything."

"And the tiara," Seb said, taking over the final part of the lesson. "It's secured well, but you've got to keep a level head—literally. No sudden bends, or you'll send it flying, and we can't have that."

I nodded, trying to absorb all their wisdom, feeling a bit like Cinderella being prepped by her fairy godmothers if her fairy godmothers were fabulous drag queens with a knack for theatrics.

"It's okay, sugar," Seb soothed my worries of a potential catastrophe. "Everything here is detachable. You can remove the train and veil after the ceremony and still celebrate with your beloved without any risk of harm."

"All right, Audrey," Mimi said, placing her hands gently on my shoulders. "Think you're ready to dazzle and not tumble?"

"I hope so," I said, "but no promises."

They all laughed, and Cherry added, "Honey, if you can handle murder mysteries, you can handle a dress. Now go out there and shine."

And so, in a dress that now told a story far richer than I ever could have imagined, I was ready to walk down the aisle.

CHAPTER NINETEEN

*S*eb had transformed my back garden into something straight out of a fairy tale. Towering trees that separated my property from the adjacent woods were now adorned with twinkling fairy lights. Strings of wisteria and ivy drooped gracefully from the branches, creating a romantic canopy. Lanterns, attached with near invisible fishing lines, floated in the space, lending a warm glow.

Potted plants of lavender, roses, and hydrangeas lined the makeshift aisle, filling the air with a fragrant bouquet. The aisle was carpeted with rose petals, leading to an elegant floral arch under which Seb stood. Comprising blooms in shades of white, blush, and deep purple, the arch was draped in gauzy fabrics that fluttered softly in the gentle breeze.

Curved rows of chairs flanked the aisle; each embellished with a lavender sprig and a ribbon. Rustic wooden tables holding an assortment of beverages and charmingly mismatched china stood ready for the post-ceremony festivities.

As the orchestral version of "At Last" by Etta James began to play, the sliding glass doors opened, and I took my first step into our makeshift but magical garden venue.

My dad stood to my right, his arm threaded through mine, and I could see the corners of his eyes crinkle as he smiled—a smile as radiant as the sunset. It warmed me through and through. But what set my heart aflutter was the presence hovering at my other side—Ben.

His form didn't just radiate a soft, celestial light —no, it was as if he'd borrowed reality itself for the day. He felt as solid and present to me as the bouquet I clutched in my hands. And it wasn't just me seeing him through the lens of memory or spiritual connection; today, he was as tactile and real as if he had never left the realm of the living. Ben looked dashing in what could best be described as a spectral tuxedo, a classic cut that would've made James Bond take notes.

I felt my eyes misting over. If life had played out differently, Ben would have stood beside me as my man of honor. He would have held the bouquet while I fumbled for my vows and probably would have had the crowd in stitches with a heartwarming yet embarrassingly honest toast.

"Looking good, Audrey," he whispered, looking as emotional as I felt. Was that a tear in his eye?

"You think?" My voice trembled, my emotions walking a tightrope.

"You were never one for fishing for compliments, but yes, you look stunning."

I took a deep breath, drawing strength from his presence. For a fleeting moment, the barrier between life and the afterlife felt paper thin, and I took it as a sign. A sign that love, friendship, and memories were energies too powerful to be constrained by such trivialities as different existential planes.

As I took my first step down the aisle, Dad on one side and the ghost of my dearest friend on the other, I knew I was the luckiest bride in the world— or perhaps, in both worlds. And as the music swelled, the crowd rose to their feet.

"Ready, love?" My dad whispered.

I glanced at Ben, who gave me a wink. "Ready as I'll ever be."

Out of the corner of my eye, I saw Emily and Rayna standing together, each wearing their wedding gowns. Their hands were clasped over their chests, and their faces were lit up with delight.

"You look beautiful, Audrey!" Emily called.

"Stunning," Rayna agreed, then nudged Emily in the ribs. "We promised we wouldn't distract her.

"Oh shoot. Right. Sorry Audrey!"

It was all I could do not to laugh.

Ahead of us were Bandit and Thor, the cutest ring bearers in the history of nuptials. Thor, wearing a tiny bow tie to make your heart melt, and Bandit in a rainbow tulle tutu, strutted—yes, strutted—down the aisle like furry little VIPs. Thor delicately held a small satin pillow in his mouth while Bandit shuffled in, expertly balancing her pillow on her upturned paw as if serving a furry feast.

As they made their way down the aisle, Bandit noticed the petals. "Ohmygosh, petals! Petals!" she squeaked, darting around to toss handfuls of petals in the air, then chase each floating piece of floral confetti. It was a spectacle—cute and hilarious.

"Bandit, come here," Kade called, bringing her attention back to the task at hand.

Thor trotted ahead, approaching Kade, who gently stroked his head and took the ring pillow from him. "Thanks, Buddy."

"I get fed now, right?" Thor said. "Seb promised treats."

"Oopsie!" Bandit remembered her mission, scampering back to the pillow she had abandoned. Gripping it tightly, she sprinted down the rest of the aisle, handing it to Kade with a look of utter devotion.

"Oh my God, aren't they the cutest?" Laura swooned, stepping in front to proceed me down the aisle, taking her place as my matron of honor, while my brother Dustin stood as Kade's best man.

And then my eyes landed on Kade.

Oh boy, did they land. He was standing at the end of the aisle, oozing an effortless elegance that took my breath away. His tan chinos fit him just right, defining his legs without screaming for attention. The rolled-up sleeves of his white button-down revealed forearms that looked like they belonged on the cover of a magazine—no gimmicks, no flash, just a perfect blend of style and substance.

The tan waistcoat he wore was the perfect touch,

framing his physique without overshadowing it. His brown hair was a swoon-inducing paradox, messy yet perfectly in place. And those gray eyes of his? They were the showstoppers. Lit with love and just a dash of mischief, as if he knew something delightful that the rest of the world didn't. As if he knew every nook and cranny of my heart and was fine with the cobwebs.

Laura had been gushing over Thor and Bandit, and rightly so, but standing there, catching Kade's eye as if tethered by an invisible force, I felt like the universe had aligned all its stars just to spell out, 'It's about darn time.'

Dad, Ben, and I stepped onto the rose-petal-strewn path, and all my anxieties about the venue, the dress, and the myriad of things that had gone wrong faded away.

Dad leaned over and murmured, "You look stunning, sweetheart. Your mom and I are so proud."

"Thank you, Dad," I whispered, grateful for their support.

Ben looked around, his eyes lingering on the gathering but inevitably returning to me. "You know, I never walked down the aisle myself, but seeing you do it—well, it feels like we're both taking that walk," he whispered, words tinged with a heartfelt sincerity only a best friend could deliver. "Everyone who should be here is here. Including me in the only way I can be."

Emotion simmering in my eyes, I leaned in close, my voice barely a whisper but loaded with the weight of a thousand unspoken words. "Ben, I can't even put into words what having you here means to me. You're not just a piece of my past; you're a cornerstone of my soul." I felt his touch, as real as the earth beneath my feet, anchoring me in this moment. "I owe you and everyone here so much more than thanks."

Taking that cautious walk down the aisle, each step was like navigating a minefield of potential disasters. Trip over a hemline here, a gush of tears there—it was a performance art piece on the edge of catastrophe. But the moment I stood beside Kade, all those hazards seemed to fade into oblivion. It wasn't just relief; it was like finding a safe harbor after a storm.

Kade cleared his throat, a shimmer of emotion in his eyes. "You look beautiful and—dare I say it —hot."

I couldn't help but chuckle, feeling my eyes moisten with emotion. "You don't look so bad yourself."

We each took a small step closer as my dad and Ben—each in his own way—relinquished their hold on me, leaving me standing next to the man I was about to spend the rest of my life with.

Seb stood before us, a radiant figure against the backdrop of my garden. He wore a rose-gold sequined jacket that caught the afternoon light, casting prismatic rainbows over the guests. Underneath, he had a crisp white shirt with ruffled cuffs peeking out flamboyantly. His trousers were tapered and black, coordinating with his patent leather Oxford shoes, which shone as if they'd been polished for days. On his left lapel was a corsage of tiny purple orchids and white lilies. His bow tie, equally showy, was an iridescent purple that complemented the flowers.

Seb was an eruption of color and flair, perfectly at home amid the elegant chaos he had orchestrated for my wedding day. From the moment he opened his mouth to welcome everyone, it was clear that Seb was in his element, doing what he did best: bringing joy, love, and a fair amount of spectacle into people's lives.

"And now, ladies and gentlemen, guests of all gender identifications and spectral entities," Seb began, casting a cheeky wink in my direction, knowing I'd appreciate the nod to Ben while leaving the guests thinking it was just his flamboyant nature. "We are gathered here today—surrounded by beauty, by nature, and let's face it, fabulousness—to unite Audrey and Kade in matrimony!"

He theatrically opened a gilded book he'd brought with him, a glimmering pen at the ready. "Marriage is a divine madness, a delightful delirium, and yes, an agreement to share popcorn on movie nights even when one of you hogs the bowl." He shot Kade an exaggeratedly accusing look. "You know who you are."

Seb leaned in closer to us, his voice dropping to a conspiratorial whisper that still carried throughout the garden. "But most of all, marriage is a promise. A promise that says, I'll be there, making coffee for you when you're running late, listening to you vent after a tough day, and occasionally letting you have the last slice of pizza. So, are we ready to make some promises?"

Kade and I nodded, our hands entwined, and Seb's face broke into a wide smile, shimmering tears at the corners of his eyes, no doubt amplified by some glitter-based product.

"Now, for the pièce de résistance, the vows. As it's

a special day, our couple has written their own." He gestured to Kade. "Kade, darling, dazzle us!"

Kade cleared his throat and looked deep into my eyes. "Audrey, do you remember the first time we met? You were the intriguing mystery about to be flattened by a bus, and I was the daring detective who leaped to your rescue. We shared a moment right then, a moment of closeness, connection, and —let's not forget—a blow to my nads."

Laughter erupted from the crowd, and I giggled along with them. "It was a love tap," I said, cutting him a sly grin.

"Ah, yes," Kade grinned back, "a love tap that doubled me over and brought me to my knees—literally. But you know what? I wouldn't change it for the world. In that vulnerable, breathless moment, I knew you were the woman who would keep me on my toes, a force to be reckoned with. I was struck by your beauty, the fierce intelligence in your eyes, and that indomitable spirit. And let's not overlook the obvious—your hotness."

The crowd chuckled again, thoroughly entertained.

Kade squeezed my hands. "You had me questioning my reality, re-evaluating my plans, and basically going, 'What the heck just happened here?' Initially, you saw me as a dirty cop, as someone not to be trusted. But here we are, and here I am, ready to dive headfirst into the intricate, wonderful, gorgeous enigma that is you. I vow to spend the rest of my life exploring every facet of your being—your strength, your heart, and, oh yeah, your undeniable hotness."

I couldn't contain my snort—Kade's grin widened, and his eyes twinkled. But apparently, he wasn't done yet.

"I vow to be your anchor in every storm, your backup on every case, and the Watson to your Sherlock—except for those times you're being overly dramatic. Then, I'll be the Lestrade who's there to remind you that you're not the only detective on the block."

A ripple of laughter sounded, and Seb gave a playful eye roll as if saying, "Only these two could mix love and law enforcement."

"I'll also vow to never let you near a stove, oven, or any kind of open flame when you're cooking. If I see you reaching for a frying pan, I'll swiftly guide you toward our trusted fire extinguisher or, better yet, a takeout menu. You'll be the only chef I know whose best dish is dialed in."

More chuckles ensued as Laura mimed a call-me gesture, already planning the next takeout order.

"And speaking of guiding, I vow to always be your GPS in life—hopefully better functioning than the one in your car that seems to have a personal vendetta against us. I'll lead you in the right direction even when the world is full of 4G black spots and GPS glitches."

Our guests grinned, their faces the very picture of entertained.

"And most importantly, Audrey, you've filled the empty pages of my life with stories I never knew I needed but now can't imagine living without. I vow to keep writing those chapters with you. You're not just another scene in my life; you're the whole darn book. And spoiler alert: in the end, we solve the mystery, nab the bad guys, and live happily ever after."

A collective "Aww" swept through the crowd. Ben rested his hand on my shoulder and whispered in my ear, "He's the one."

Seb's grin almost outshone the setting sun. He gestured at me. "All right, Audrey, your turn to give it your best shot, no pressure or anything."

I cleared my throat and looked into Kade's eyes, a twinkle of mischief brewing. "Kade, our first meeting was, to put it mildly, a hit—literally. I recall the blaring horn of the bus, the lurch of panic, and then you—leaping in like a modern-day Superman, minus the cape. We slammed heads so hard, I think you knocked some sense into both of us." I winked.

The audience chuckled, some with raised brows, enjoying our banter.

"But we have Ben to thank for that, don't we?" I cast a glance at where Ben stood by my side, invisible to everyone but me. "Without a doubt, he would be standing right here as my man of honor if heaven hadn't needed him back so soon."

The atmosphere thickened, weighted with the gravity of the sentiment.

"But back to us and our clumsy, fate-laden collision. Our first accidental grope was to your family jewels, no less. Nothing says 'Hello' like a surprise uppercut to the nether regions, right?" I said, a grin slowly spreading across my face.

Laughter wafted in the air, punctuated by a few snorts and a high-pitched giggle. I paused, waiting for the laughter to die down.

"Kade, that moment was the universe slapping me awake, making me notice you—not just as another face in the crowd, but as the one face I couldn't live without. Sure, I had my doubts. But you broke down my walls. You didn't just look at me; you saw me. The real me. And that's the reason why I'm standing here today. That's the reason I can't wait to spend the rest of my life as your loving, if somewhat clumsy, wife."

I sucked in a trembling breath, my heart so full I feared it would burst.

"I vow to be your partner in crime and in life. You're the Watson to my Holmes, the caffeine to my mornings—oh, and speaking of mornings, you're on coffee duty—and yes, I know I make a pretty good brew, but let's be real, we both know I function better when I'm fully caffeinated. So I vow to let you make the morning coffee because love is ... sharing the responsibility of my caffeine fix."

Kade interjected, "I couldn't agree more. Honestly, I love your caffeine-fueled, clumsy ways. It adds excitement to every scene of our life, like a twist nobody saw coming. Keeps me on my toes— sometimes literally when you're rushing around!"

Chuckles rippled through the crowd once more.

I grinned, "And speaking of toes, I'm in total agreement. I vow to avoid any and all cooking tasks involving fire. If you ever see me reaching for a frying pan, kindly point me towards a microwave or a takeout menu."

I paused, grinning at the gathered crowd before focusing on Kade again. "Taking that initial leap of faith with you was the most terrifying and exhilarating moment of my life. I vow to take more leaps, make more memories, and solve more mysteries—with you, for you, because of you. And above all, I don't ever want to look back on my life and think ... what could've been, what should've been. You, Kade Galloway, are my forever case and one that I'll gladly spend a lifetime cracking."

The air between us seemed to shimmer with the weight of our words, our promises hanging in the space, as real as if they'd been written in the sky.

Seb, ever the conductor of human emotion, knew exactly when to cut in. "Oh, you two. Could you be any more perfect? Even *my* mascara is running." Seb dabbed his eyes with an ornate handkerchief. Flipping the page in his glittering book, he continued. "All right, lovelies, let's make this thing official. Who needs legality when you've got love? Am I right? But we'll do it for the paperwork."

Kade and I nodded, our hands still intertwined, the heat of our promises still glowing between us.

Seb theatrically cleared his throat. "Do you, Kade Xavier Galloway, take Audrey Gertha

Fitzgerald—yes, we're pulling out all the stops with full names today—to have and to hold, in good times and bad, in sickness and health, and various states of caffeine deprivation?"

My cheeks flushed at the mention of my middle name. Oh, he went there.

Feigning shock, Seb turned to me. "Gertha? Seriously? You made it sound like a relic from the medieval dungeon of names. Honestly, I kinda dig it."

The crowd giggled, and my desire to evaporate intensified.

Seb winked at me and nodded toward my mom. "Right, Mom? Gertha's like the Wonder Twins of Bertha and Gertrude, yeah?"

Mom shot back a thumbs-up. "It's a legacy of her grandmothers," she confirmed, her smile blooming.

Seb turned back to the crowd. "See, not so terrible. It's unique, just like our one-and-only Audrey. Now, let's get back to the I do's and I-will's, shall we?"

Laughter erupted again, and this time, I joined in. If Gertha had to take center stage, my wedding was the perfect venue.

"Do you, Kade Xavier Galloway, take Audrey Gertha Fitzgerald to have and to hold, in good times and in bad, in sickness and in health, and in various states of caffeine deprivation?"

Kade's eyes twinkled. "I do, and the coffeemaker's already set for our first morning as Mr. and Mrs. Caffeinated."

Seb laughed. "A man with priorities. Love it."

He swiveled to me. "And you, Audrey Gertha Fitzgerald, do you take this coffee-obsessed, dashing, and yes, popcorn-monopolizing man, Kade Xavier Galloway, to be your lawfully wedded husband?"

Tears welled up, but I locked eyes with Kade. "I do. And I've got our first dinner as newlyweds sorted —takeout menus at the ready."

Seb dramatically raised his arms. "By the powers vested in me by the internet, romance, and my innate ability to steal the show, I now pronounce you partners in crime and caffeine. You may now kiss!"

As our lips met, joy ricocheted through every fiber of my being. This was it: Audrey, the queen of klutzes, and Kade, the patron saint of patience, joined in marital—and comical—bliss. And not to forget our fur-kids, Bandit and Thor, who'd continue to bring the right amount of chaos into our perfectly imperfect life.

I couldn't have been happier to waltz—or, let's be honest, stumble—into this new chapter.

EPILOGUE

*T*he sun had bowed out for the day, leaving a cloak of darkness punctuated by the fairy lights that dangled from the trees like little glowing orbs. It was a scene straight out of a fairy tale—only better because the fairytale didn't have our playlist.

The reception was in full swing, and the dance floor had turned into a kaleidoscope of joyous mayhem. Ben was at the center, nimbly wheeling himself in circles, surrounded by Emily and Rayna. Our incorporeal guests were having the time of their un-alive lives! As the beat dropped, Brad grabbed Laura's hand, pulling her into an astonishing pirouette. Not to be outdone, our drag queen friends

were seriously schooling everyone on how to own a
dance floor.

"Everyone's having a great time," Kade
whispered, nudging me as we watched from the
sidelines.

"I had no idea Brad could dance like that," I
replied, my eyes wide with pride and awe, thrilled
everyone was enjoying themselves.

The playlist suddenly switched tracks, filling the
air with the sappy notes of a timeless love ballad.
Kade extended his hand, and with a goofy grin, I
took it.

As we joined the dance floor, I looked around at
the people who filled our lives with love, laughter,
and a sprinkling of chaos. We had friends who were
more like family and a love that felt like it had been
written in the stars.

"What's our next move, partner in crime?" Kade
grinned, pulling me close as we spun around on the
dance floor.

"First order of business—cake!" I announced.

Hand in hand, we sauntered over to the cake
table, where our stunning three-tiered marvel stood
proudly. This bad boy was a country-chic dream,
wrapped in fondant and crowned with a bouquet of

edible wildflowers. A true culinary ode to our rustic setting.

As Kade reached for the knife, our world turned into an animal version of 'Fast and Furious.' With the stealth of four-legged ninjas, Bandit and Thor blitzed toward the cake. Before we could say "paw-don you," they swiped a generous chunk of frosting and cake from the bottom tier.

My eyes widened, and I turned to Kade, who was already in a state of amused disbelief. "Well, looks like the cake-tasting committee has a couple of furry members."

Kade chuckled, shaking his head. "Is it bad that I'm kind of proud of their impeccable timing? Look at them go!"

Sure enough, one overweight cat and one cute as a button raccoon were already savoring their stolen loot a safe distance away, their fur covered in frosting with zero regrets.

I laughed, glancing up at Kade. "As long as they leave some for us, I'm fine with it."

Regaining our composure, Kade and I returned our attention to the cake—what was left of it, anyway. There was a momentary hush from the crowd, the sort of sacred silence that only happens when you're about to decimate something beautiful for a darn good reason. With our hands overlapping on the knife handle, we took a deep, synchronized breath.

"Ready?" Kade whispered, his eyes twinkling like he was about to reveal the secret of the universe—or at least, the secret to not botching our cake-cutting moment.

"Ready," I echoed, squeezing his hand as we plunged the knife into the cake, skirting around the paw-missing segment like pros.

The crowd erupted into cheers as we triumphantly lifted a slice. Instead of the standard, photo-ready moment where we'd daintily feed each other, Kade mischievously smeared a little frosting on my nose. I laughed and retaliated with a dollop of frosting on his cheek.

"Ah, the sweet taste of matrimony," Kade grinned, finally offering me a proper bite.

I looked around as I tasted the cake—a sinful concoction of vanilla, berries, and rebellion. Here we were, icing on our faces, surrounded by the people who were the cornerstones of our crazy, unpredictable, and utterly wonderful life. It struck me then, as I caught the approving nod from Ben's spectral form and a nodding head from Bandit that I wouldn't trade this beautiful mess for anything in the world.

As I savored the last crumbs of cake, I leaned in to whisper something lovey-dovey in Kade's ear. But my heel caught on a decorative ribbon from the tablecloth, pulling it taut. Before I knew it, I was stumbling forward, arms flailing like a newly hatched flamingo learning to walk. My eyes widened; I was going down, and that gorgeous, almost entirely intact wedding cake was about to get a full-faced Audrey imprint.

But faster than you could say, 'marital disaster,' Kade swooped in, arms firm around my waist, pulling me back into a standing position. The cake remained untouched—or, at least, no more touched than it had been by our four-legged cake tasters.

The crowd gasped, then burst into laughter and applause. Even Amanda had to clap for that save.

"Ah, there's the Audrey trademark we've been waiting for," Kade chuckled, steadying me with both hands now. "The day just wouldn't be complete without it."

I looked up at him, my eyes twinkling with love and a touch of embarrassment. "I promise, not all of our marital milestones will involve near-cake catastrophes."

Kade leaned down and kissed me, frosting and all. "Even if they do, I wouldn't miss them for the world."

Just then, Amanda sashayed toward us, her eyes narrowing as she took in the spectacle of love and hilarity.

"Audrey," she sniffed, touching her pearl necklace as if to steady herself. "Don't you think your reception is a smidgen... eclectic?" Her eyes flickered to the drag queens, to Thor and Bandit's cake heist, and then to Seb, who was having a dance-off... with himself.

I glanced at Kade, who shrugged, his eyes twinkling. "Your call, love," he mouthed.

I turned back to Amanda. "Eclectic? No, Amanda, it's authentically us—filled with people we love and who love us back, and that's more than enough. I'd rather have this 'eclectic' mess than a perfectly polished borefest any day."

A collective "ooh" went up from the crowd, who'd been eavesdropping just a teensy bit. Amanda flushed, mumbled something about refreshing her drink, and hurried off.

Kade wrapped an arm around me and leaned in, his lips a whisper away from mine. "You've wanted to put that into words for years, haven't you?"

I grinned back, my heart feeling as full as the dance floor. "Ah, Kade, you don't know the half of it. But she's still family. A prickly pear in a patch of wildflowers, but still."

He chuckled, giving me a peck that tasted like cake and love and forever. "That's the Audrey I fell head over heels for, always seeing the good in everyone, even when they're hell-bent on changing you."

Kade pulled me back in for a dance. As our friends and family swayed to the music around us— some alive, some spectral—I felt an overwhelming sense of warmth and gratitude.

Here we were: Audrey Gertha Fitzgerald and Kade Xavier Galloway—partners in love, in chaos, and now, in cake-tasting triumphs. The truth was, there was no other mystery I'd rather spend my life solving.

The end? Nah, this was just the beginning.

Are you a fan of the Ghost Detective mysteries? Sign up for my newsletter and receive two bonus Ghost Detective shorts!

www.janehinchey.com/ghostly-newsflash

READ MORE BY JANE

Find them all at www.JaneHinchey.com/books

The Ghost Detective Mysteries

#1 Ghost Mortem

#2 Give up the Ghost

#3 The Ghost is Clear

#4 A Ghost of a Chance

#5 Here Ghost Nothing

#6 Who Ghost There?

#7 Wild Ghost Chase

#8 Easy Come, Easy Ghost

#9 Life Ghost On

Witch Way Paranormal Cozy Mystery Series

#1 Witch Way to Magic & Mayhem

#2 Witch Way to Romance & Ruin

#3 Witch Way Down Under

#4 Witch Way to Beauty & the Beach

#5 Witch Way to Death & Destruction

ABOUT JANE

Hi there! My name is Jane and I write urban fantasy romance and paranormal cozy mysteries, but let's be real, I'm just trying to figure out how to make my love for cats, coffee, and romance a career.

My hobbies include trying to outsmart my cats, getting lost in a good book, and pretending to be a plant lady (but really, I just have a lot of plastic plants).

In my free time, you can find me binge-watching true crime documentaries, planning my next vacation, and perfecting my "resting book face." I am also a big believer in the power of naps and have been known to take them at any given opportunity.

I also have a not-so-secret identity as an author of steamy and badass urban fantasy romance under the name Zahra Stone, so if you're looking for a little more danger and a lot more heat, check her out!

Find Zahra here: www.zahrastone.com

Find me (Jane) here: www.janehinchey.com

Printed in the USA
CPSIA information can be obtained
at www.ICGtesting.com
LVHW051438121123
763715LV00040B/437